DYING IS NO
BIG DEAL

To Hank and Rita Eber.
thanks, and thanks for that
great son, Hank they # they Joehg
e Joseph

DYING IS NO BIG DEAL

And other VISUAL stories

C. Joseph Socha

Library of Congress Number: 2002093677
ISBN :   Hardcover   1-4010-6896-0
                 Softcover   1-4010-6895-2

This book was printed in the United States of America.

To order additional copies of this book, contact:
Xlibris Corporation
1-888-795-4274
www.Xlibris.com
Orders@Xlibris.com
16056

CONTENTS

DEDICATION

To my wife Emilie of 47 years and son Paul Michael
who departed too soon to share this work with me.

Also

to daughters Glorianne Terese, Michelle Annette,
Marie Lenore, and Mary Socha

And

to those special angels, Henry Ebel, David Skridulis,
Toni and Ron Wilbanks, and Cathy Coon.

ALSO BY C. JOSEPH SOCHA

"Don't Call Me Clarence"
(An Autobiography)

"Promise"
(A Novel)

SOMETHING MORE

Some of us cannot be content
Merely to be what we seem meant
To be; we will not settle for
What seems; we must be something more!
Something in us makes us feel,
What seems is not what is really real.
Friend, you and I have hidden powers
Past any we have dreamed were ours;
Let no one say, "This is your lot!"
Something there is in you and me
That links us with Infinity,
And who can say what we may be!

James Dillet Freeman

INTRODUCTION

"Dying Is No Big Deal" is the title of one of the stories in this book. It was an international short story contest winner and titles this book. In all the stories here, the author uses a technique he calls VISUAL writing which he developed as an audio-visual copywriter. He began his writing career with an agency that produced slide films, motion pictures and product announcement stage productions. The emphasis was on *seeing* a product in use, of people, models shown in product-use situations. Pictures were all-important in that expensive medium and required considerable planning and refining so that what was shown on the screen, or in the printed medium, came as close as possible to hauling the audience to the actual scene of action. So Socha learned to write VISUAL copy and advanced in his commercial writing skills.

The author's writing was also influenced by his experience during the Great Depression. There was no TV. Family entertainment consisted of turning the lights low and listening to the radio commentator, and dramatists, describe what was happening—and the listeners *visualized* what was taking place. And so the listeners *saw* the Lone Ranger in their minds. They *visualized* Jack Benny, Fibber McGee and Molly, Edgar Bergen and Charlie McCarthy, and, never to be forgotten, they participated in that sensational Orson Welles' radio drama in 1937 of "The Invasion of The Martians." That drama was so real that it caused panic among listeners; some even armed themselves to fight the Martians. VISUAL entertainment. Powerful!

What is different about audio-visual writing? The *camera*. The writer is conscious that he is *showing* what is happening—to register this on the reader's mind. Like an establishing long shot introducing the people, the place, the action, then various close-ups where the characters reveal themselves and their feelings. There is more action in audio-visual writing. For example, in the opening sequence of the author's novel, "Promise," the action is instantaneous and continuous, like a newsreel. The stories in "Dying Is No Big Deal" are much like that—like video dramas.

In the beginning of his career, as an apprentice writer, Socha went on location with photographic crews and models and saw how the director produced what a shooting script called for. He saw how actors were selected to enhance the action. It was revealing to observe how actors were transformed adhering to the shooting script, when told who they were to be in the story and what they would say. Especially memorable was the author's observation of an automobile company's product announcement show being produced by this agency and using Broadway talent. One of the stars was a timid actor, extremely self-conscious and uncomfortable outside her role, but when she was called before the camera to do her part, she transformed into the most animated, delightful, and sexy dancer and singer that the author had ever seen. All the pieces fit the visual plan.

Visual writing enhanced the author's creative stimulus. The picture in the writer's mind of an idea, of characters, of plot, started the writing process. Once the idea was there, the characters sought expression, and the copy rushed to a necessary conclusion. The writer's fingers flashed over the typewriter keyboard as fast as the mind produced the movement. All the stories in this book began with a picture in mind, something that captured the writer's imagination and stimulated the process. Preceding each story here is a comment about what inspired a story. Sometimes the starting thought was only a small part of the total story that resulted. That's what happened in "Freedom Tree." Socha and a fellow writer at the Ross Roy agency in Detroit, ate their lunch on the roof of the office building where they watched the boat traffic on the Detroit River several blocks away. It was a pleasant break in the day. One day they saw a tiny poplar seedling growing in a crack of tarpaper roofing. No way could it survive there without nourishment, but it seemed determined to live. Inspiring! Several years later the thought of that struggling seedling became part of "Freedom Tree." The story "Glow" was inspired by a beautiful clerk Socha saw in a tiny used book store. How could he work her into a story? How about this? She is pregnant, unmarried, and this young writer shopping in her store falls in love with her.

Then there is "Dying Is No Big Deal." It is about a self-serving, conniving business executive who takes advantage of the skills of the story's hero. The executive benefits from the hero's skills then fires him. There is exciting action involving an amoral, criminal character, and a surprise ending.

"Merry Christmas. This Is A Stick-up" had an interesting beginning. Socha had been visiting his mother-in-law in a nursing home. Conditions there were depressing, but what if there were a couple of kooky characters to liven things up? Humor from a sad situation? There always were possibilities.

There are seventeen stories in this book with a variety of plots about people in everyday situations. The variety should appeal to almost every reader's interest: Humor, romance, sports, psychological. Several stories will surely create a lot of discussion, for instance, "The Fish Who Loved Old Grandad." It is about two inept fishermen who desperately try to prove themselves. Fishermen will get a kick out of this one.

Writing is an exciting experience. Story ideas pop up everywhere. Say you get on a bus and watch people coming and going. Their faces are blank as they are in deep thought. Any story there? Well, no, but then ahhh! There is this beautiful redhead sitting across, reading a book. Legs! Million-dollar legs! A gorgeous lady. She could certainly inspire a story. The writer closes his eyes and is mentally constructing a story and a lascivious expression appears on his face. Oh, oh! She glances over. A bit embarrassing. Can she read what's on his mind? If she could, maybe it could lead to yet another story.

Writing can be therapeutic. Certainly. Say the writer finds himself in a sad mood. He is feeling dissatisfied with the way his life is going. Suddenly he perks up. Visualizes a situation where he, his character, becomes a successful, dashing hero. He's not a sad Socha anymore. He is the hero in a story. Not only does this change his attitude about himself, but he's creating a story that might sell! What a way to make a living!

THE ANGEL GABRIELLE *

There really was a Miss Gabrielle, an intermediate school English teacher who recognized my creative ability and encouraged me to join The young Writer's Club. She inspired me to become a professional writer.

Richard Milliken couldn't get Miss Gabrielle out of his mind. He'd given her such a hard time in school. That was twenty-five years ago, of course, but as he drove through his old hometown this morning, he felt a strong desire to look her up.

He laughed at his impulsiveness. Miss Gabrielle probably wouldn't recognize him or remember him as the problem child who sat in the back row of her class at Cleveland Intermediate. Still, it might be interesting to see her, to show her how far he'd come since those days.

Once he'd made the decision, the urge became stronger. He drove to his old school and walked into the building. He felt strange and sad at the same time as he made his way through the loud, irrepressible children rushing through the halls.

"Miss Gabrielle?" the office clerk echoed. "We have no teacher by that name. Are you sure you have the right school?"

Of course she wasn't here now. She must be at least seventy. "I know she's not here," Richard said. "She taught my English class twenty-five years ago. I just wondered if you might know where she lives today."

The principal overheard the discussion and remembered. "Oh, yes. Angel Gabrielle, we used to call her."

Richard laughed. Yes, that's what they called her. He'd almost forgotten. "Do you have any idea where she lives?"

The principal promised to check into it. Richard left his motel

17

telephone number with her then walked down the hall and up the worn stairs to Room 215.

The classroom looked more cheerful today than he'd remembered. The furniture was brightly colored and the walls were painted in soft pastels. He watched the teacher who stood at the chalkboard, going over verb tenses. The children looked bored. In the back row, a few students were carrying on a conversation of their own. Things hadn't really changed that much.

Back in his car, Richard drove to his old neighborhood. Main Street was depressingly deteriorated—deserted buildings, some burned out, others covered with ominous steel bars as protection against break-ins. The street where he grew up was barely recognizable. Half the homes were torn down, leaving in their place empty lots overgrown with weeds. Others were abandoned and boarded up.

The house where he had lived was one of the abandoned ones. He got out of his car and walked over broken glass and debris to the front porch. The stairs were gone. Around the side, all the windows were broken. The rear door was partly boarded up, but he was able to squeeze inside. He made his way across the litter, through the dining room, into the living room, and then to his old bedroom. Unexpected tears burned his eyes. "My God!" he sobbed. "I've got to get out of here."

He walked back into the living room and peeked through the cracks in the boards to the front porch. He had spent many happy days on that porch—reading, studying, dreaming. The memory led his thoughts right back to Miss Gabrielle.

His had been an especially disruptive class—partly because either Miss Gabrielle was hard of hearing or she just ignored the noise. "Hark!" she used to say to quiet the class. It was never "Quiet!" or "Attention!" It was always "Hark!" That was how she got her nickname, Angel Gabrielle. It came from the song, "Hark, the Herald Angels Sing."

Miss Gabrielle was the ugliest person Richard had ever known. She was six feet tall, maybe taller—or so it seemed to him when he was twelve. She had a terrible complexion. Her face was fat and puffy and pockmarked. Her teeth were huge and protruded over her lower lip. The kids neighed like horses, making obvious references to her teeth. Her dull, colorless hair was always combed back into a bun. She dressed in old ladies' clothes—dull, patterned dresses, and black, low-heeled shoes.

Although Miss Gabrielle remained passive through the confusion and noise in her class, she had at least a dozen times grabbed Richard by his ear and ushered him down to the principal's office for being impertinent, obstinate, and for creating a class disturbance.

There was a turning point, however.

Richard was a terrible student in just about every class, but English was the pits. Miss Gabrielle told him he was getting an F and would not pass to the next grade. And, she assured him, she would not give him a D just so he could move up a grade. He would either shape up or fail.

Richard's parents were brought into the act. His father and mother both worked. They spent very little time overseeing Richard's studies. Until Miss Gabrielle's note came along, there had been no need. His other teachers had been more tolerant of his performance. They were probably glad to pass him on to the next grade just to get rid of him.

But not Miss Gabrielle!

Miss Gabrielle offered to stay after school to help Richard upgrade his marks. He remembered their first session. Miss Gabrielle motioned for him to sit in the row directly in front of her desk. She looked at him for a long moment. Richard defiantly tried to stare her down.

"Now look, young man," she had said. "I don't relish staying after school, and I wouldn't even bother except," she leaned forward on her elbows and looked straight into his eyes, "except that you are an intelligent boy. You have great potential. You could amount to something someday. But you are aggressive and stubborn and arrogant. Now what's your problem?"

"I don't have a problem."

"Oh, yes, you do! You are getting a failing grade, but that's not the sad part. The sad part is you could be an A student. I've seen your compositions. You have a poor grasp of grammar and spelling, but your ideas are brilliant. I know the routine. If you fail, you'll be in the same class next term. The others will tease you about being stupid. That will add to your feelings of anger and will carry over into your entire life. I plan to prevent that if I have to pull your ears off your head. Now sit up and pay attention!"

The look she'd given him was scary. Richard gulped and sat up.

"Do you like to read?" she'd asked.

"Reading's for sissies."

Miss Gabrielle had nodded, but Richard was sure she didn't understand. He lived in a tough neighborhood. Many of the guys on his street were already in reform school. Street fights broke out regularly, and Richard was usually involved. If the guys thought for a minute that he'd gone soft, his life could become a living hell.

"Do you like dogs?" Miss Gabrielle had asked then.

Now where was she coming from? Richard had wondered. But he'd just said, "Sure."

Miss Gabrielle handed him a book from the school library—*Lad* by Albert Payson Terhune. "Your homework for tonight is to read three chapters of this book. Tomorrow I will test you on those chapters."

So Richard had read the book. It wasn't easy but it was interesting—very interesting! In fact, he'd read six chapters on that first night (of course, he didn't tell Miss Gabrielle that).

The next day he tried to convince her that he hated the book and pretended not to remember or understand it when she questioned him.

Richard finished the entire book over the weekend. On Monday, he went to the school library and took out *Wolf,* another Terhune book. He didn't mention that to Miss Gabrielle either. During the time they were plodding along on Lad, Richard actually read two other Terhune books on his own.

Then Miss Gabrielle brought him a book about Kit Carson. He read that one in two evenings. Soon he was secretly reading three books a week. Miss Gabrielle was pleased with his progress. When she assigned the class to write a short story on any subject, Richard wrote one entitled "Kit Frankton, Hero Scout."

"Very good," Miss Gabrielle had said, calling attention to parts of the story that were outstanding as well as to parts that needed work. By the end of that term, Richard had a B in English—the highest mark he had ever received.

Richard passed on to the next grade. Although Miss Gabrielle was no longer his teacher, she would stop him in the hall occasionally to inquire how he was doing and ask if he was reading any interesting books. "Nah," he'd reply. "Reading's for sissies."

Although it didn't occur to him then, he later discovered that Miss Gabrielle had been checking with the librarian and suggesting books that might help move him along into more advanced reading.

Miss Gabrielle also persuaded Richard to join the school's chapter of the Young Writers' Club, sponsored by the local newspaper to encourage youthful expression. He became its most prolific contributor. In fact, his work had helped the school win the annual Young Writers' Award two years in a row.

When Richard moved on to high school, he dropped by to chat with Miss Gabrielle occasionally, seeking her advice on writing assignments or discussing whatever books he had been reading.

After high school, Richard took college evening classes, majoring in English and journalism. When he earned his degree, one of the first things he did was to stop by the school to tell Miss Gabrielle. She was vacationing in Europe.

The setting sun and the darkness in the abandoned house startled Richard back to the present. He returned to his motel. There was a message from the school principal waiting for him at the desk. Miss Gabrielle, the message informed him, was in a nursing home on the West Side. She'd had a stroke but could have visitors. Richard drove to the nursing home the next morning.

Miss Gabrielle shared a room with another resident. It was a drab cell, smelling of stale urine and disinfectant. She was sitting in a wheelchair by the window, examining the African violets on the sill. He hardly recognized her.

He stood beside her. "Miss Gabrielle?" She looked up, blinking. "My name is Richard Milliken."

She nodded affirmatively. Richard could see that the left side of her face was paralyzed. "Richard! I remember you."

In spite of the years and his extra pounds and the loss of hair, she recognized him! He searched for words. He certainly couldn't ask, "How are you?" That was obvious. She smiled. "And what have you done with yourself, Richard?"

"I'm a newspaper reporter. A feature writer."

She nodded and smiled again.

He felt stifled by the odors in the room. "Can I take you for a stroll outdoors? It's such a beautiful day."

"I don't want to trouble you," she answered.

"No trouble. I'd like very much to do that."

Outdoors, they strolled to the picnic area and stopped at a bench next to a fountain that splashed into a pool with goldfish in it. They sat and watched the water cascade.

She tilted her head at the sound of a bird. "Hark!" she said. "A cardinal. I always loved the song of the cardinal."

They both fell silent again, listening to the running water and the bird's song, each captured in a private place of memory.

After a while, Miss Gabrielle broke the silence. "Please, take me indoors, Richard. I get tired so quickly."

Back in her room he helped her into her bed and closed the blinds. She looked up then and asked, "Do you live in town?"

"No, just passing through. I'm leaving tonight."

"Well, I'm proud of you, Richard Milliken. You turned out all right."

"I just wanted you to know that I love you for what you did for me."

Tears formed in her eyes, welled up, and rolled down her face. "Good-bye, Richard. Thank you for coming."

Then the Angel Gabrielle closed her eyes and went to sleep.

Notes

* Originally published in Liguorian September 1987. Reprinted with permission from Liguorian, 1 Ligurian Drive, Liguori, MO 63057.

CARING PEOPLE

During one of those severe recessions in Detroit, people were desperate. The main character, ashamed at not providing for his family, embarks on a journey to find work.

Being married to Carl Cramer was all that Marie had prayed for. Carl was a loving husband, a happy person! He had a great sense of humor. And he was a hard-working, trusting man. When she became pregnant, Carl treated her like a delicate princess. And when Elenna was born, no one loved a child more than Carl.

When Elenna was eighteen months old, she became ill. The doctors said it was serious, but Carl refused to accept this. He stopped at the church every day before and after work to pray for her. But the baby's condition worsened. One night, as Carl rocked Elenna to sleep and sang her a lullaby, she died in his arms.

Marie tried to comfort Carl but he carried his burden within himself. He seldom smiled. He stopped going to church and became withdrawn and cynical. Even after Joseph and Edward were born and they seemed happy again, Carl never let go the pain.

The boys grew and it appeared that Carl showed signs of regaining his old self. But he was so protective of the children that Marie feared this might destroy their confidence in themselves. Carl appeared to have built a fortress, a defense against the world outside. "Never again will anything hurt this family. I'll see to that! We don't need anybody. We'll take care of ourselves!"

Then came the terrible recession. Carl had never been out of work. Even in previous recessions he managed to provide, at times working several jobs. But this time his factory closed down. Unemployment compensation ran out. Carl worked several minimum-wage jobs but the bills exceeded income. They lost their automobile, then the house. They were forced to live with Marie's widowed mother.

"There must be some place in this country where we can live with more security," Carl told Marie. "I won't permit you and the children to suffer this anymore."

Carl persuaded his friends, Fred Schultz and Marty Morger, who faced the same problems, to seek work elsewhere. They scanned the trade journals and out-of-town classified ads and made a list of cities where opportunities seemed promising. They would use Fred Schultz's six-year-old Ford station wagon and share costs. The wagon was large enough for them to sleep in overnight to save money.

Carl said his goodbyes to Marie and the children. There was a lot of crying and hugging. Carl had difficulty letting go of them. "I'll be back for you soon," he promised.

After two weeks on the road, Fred and Marty decided to give up. "You can't quit now, for gosh sakes," Carl pleaded. "Opportunity could be right around the corner."

"We're leaving, Carl," Fred Schultz said. "You want to keep going then go ahead."

Carl watched them drive away. He pointed his thumb southward and continued. He worked any job he could find to keep going—dishwasher, car wash, short-order cook. They fired him at the restaurant because he really did not know how to cook, but he got a good breakfast and lunch out of it.

What little money he could spare Carl sent to Marie. "I'll see you soon," he wrote. "Hugs and kisses."

On Thanksgiving Day he was forced to eat at a charity hall. He had difficulty swallowing the food. How far down could one go? That night he slept in a county park, covering himself with newspapers that he found in a trash basket.

Next morning he read the classified section of the newspapers that served as his blanket. A large display ad offered construction work in Albuquerque. He decided to go there. It was a long way off but closer than home.

He had a breakfast of eggs, toast and coffee in a diner at the edge of town. He felt invigorated but was now only fifty-cents rich. That was all right. He was going to find a job.

Just outside of town on a mountain road the weather turned on him. It rained hard and the wind grew gusty and cold. He hiked all day with only a few short rides. By nightfall he was a long way from shelter. Though it seemed impossible, it began to rain harder. Where would he sleep this night? Then he saw it, briefly, in a flash of lightning—a dilapidated shanty setting on the edge of the mountain road.

He slogged through the mud toward the shanty. No one inside. He briefly considered the safety of the tottering shack as it rocked beneath his weight. Not much choice, he thought, and sank to his knees exhausted.

Carl closed his eyes and visualized Marie and the family eating dinner. There would be that empty chair, his. He clasped his hands together to pray but stopped. "No. That doesn't help. I'll do it alone. I don't need anybody!" Feeling the sting of tears, he shook his head. "Nobody cares," he cried and sagged to the floor and fell asleep.

It rained throughout the night. A pool of water formed on the land upon which the shanty sat. The water covered Carl's tracks, then crept higher, reaching the shanty's porch. A steady stream crossed the road swelling the pool around the shack.

The first shifting of earth came shortly after dawn. Loose rocks slid down into the ravine nearly a thousand feet below. Then, it seemed that the entire mountain disintegrated, sinking, sliding downward with a roar.

Carl felt himself being lifted and thrown across the room. He clawed at the floor and watched furniture slide past him and crash through the wall leaving an open end in the shanty. A heavy joist had fallen on him, pinning him down, fortunately preventing him from sliding out with the furniture through the open end. In this violent awakening Carl saw a desk and chairs hurtling down into the chasm.

What kept the shack from going down? Through half of the roof that was gone he saw a thin, frayed wire tautly tied to a pole across the road. "Come on, God! Don't let that wire snap!" The rain poured through the roof opening onto his face. Above, an angry sky. Below, a long, long way down. Carl groaned. "God, what have I done to deserve this?"

His eyes followed the joist on his chest. It lay across the room, wedged against the opposite wall—all that kept the two sides from caving in. If it swung free, he would follow the furniture to the bottom.

Then he thought he heard a voice. That's all he needed: hallucination. It was a woman's voice. "Hello. Hello."

"Hello," he ventured.

"Hello!" The voice was impatient. "Will someone please answer? Or hang up!" It was someone on a phone. Ridiculous place for a phone!

Turning his head toward the voice he saw the phone receiver dangling out of reach above his head. "Can you hear me?" he shouted.

"Who is it?"

"Send help. Help."

"What's wrong there?"

"Landslide. I'm trapped in a shanty and it's about to slide down the mountain."

The back of his legs hurt terribly as he tensed against the floor. He dug his heels into the floor and kept his back and shoulders flat, providing as much friction as possible.

He wondered about the voice. It had stopped. If the rain continued, he knew more of the mountain would slide down. Even if it didn't, he could not hold on much longer. He felt himself slipping.

"Are you there?" The voice was back.

"Where else?" he groaned. His muscles twitched. Heck, he'd never make it!

"Where are you from?" It was a pleasant voice. Young. It tried to sound casual but he detected urgency.

"Detroit," he said.

"I'm from Cincinnati. Came about nine years ago."

His muscles cramped. The pain was excruciating. He must keep his mind off it. Talk to the voice. Anything. She had a very young voice. "You know what I was doing when I was your age?" he asked. "Loading trucks. Twelve hours a day."

"That must have been very hard work," she said.

He shifted his body cautiously. The ache spread throughout his back and neck and throbbed like hundreds of electrical shocks. He moaned.

"You remind me of my father," the voice said. "He kept telling me how hard he worked when he was my age."

Carl shook his head but this did not lessen the pain. He looked through the open end of the shack. It nauseated him. It could be over quickly. Just shove that joist, close the eyes and go. "Hey. Hey. Can you hear me?" he shouted.

"I can hear you."

"Please take a message. For my wife."

"Oh come on, mister. Help is on the way. Just a little longer."

"Kid, I can't. I just can't."

She kept talking. He took a deep breath. He would close his eyes and shove that joist free.

The voice was crying, pleading. Why should she care? Why should anyone?

His mind wandered. He was considering a strange sight. Momentarily he forgot what it was but it persisted. He tried remembering what it was. A ladder moving? Someone on a seat. A chair hovering above him . . . a strange apparition he could see through the hole in the roof. A strange voice, guttural, excited. It was not talking to Carl. It was yelling directions to someone.

The girl's voice came again. "Mister. Mister. Please hold on. Just a few minutes more. Please."

"Kid," he shouted to her. "Relax. I've got company."

"Thank God!"

After they got Carl out, a telephone lineman clipped the wires that held the shack. It went tumbling down the mountain, scattering into splinters.

"Whew!" Carl exhaled. The full impact of his ordeal made his body twitch and tremble. He looked around. There was an army of people there in the rain. Firemen, police, spectators. A fortune in manpower and equipment to save one man with only a half a buck in his jeans.

A reporter with a camera approached. "I'm from the local newspaper. Mind if we talk and take some pictures?"

Then Carl saw her. She stood near the reporter's automobile—a slender girl in a raincoat, her arms folded around herself. She was crying and shaking.

"Is that the voice?" he asked the reporter.

"Yeah. Poor kid was so shook up they told her to go home. But she wanted to make sure you were all right."

Carl walked toward her. Her eyes widened. And then she ran to him and they threw their arms around each other. "Thank God!" she kept saying. "Thank God!"

"What's your name?" Carl asked.

"Helen. Helen Wierzbicki."

He laughed. "How do you spell it?"

The reporter watched. "You know, that shanty's floor was nearly vertical when they got to you. How did you manage to hold on so long?"

Carl thought about it. "My family," he said. "I have a wonderful family." And he tightened his arms around Helen, "And people who care. Helen could have shrugged it off. Why worry about some down-and-out drifter? What did it matter, right?"

"It matters," Helen's voice, muffled against Carl's chest, said. "It matters."

A foreman from the construction company that owned the shanty approached. "You all right?"

"Still kicking," Carl said. "Thanks to all of you."

Helen insisted that they stop at St. Mary's Church. Carl wanted to wait outside but Helen took his hand and they all went in. Carl and the reporter sat in the back pew while Helen walked to the altar. She lit two candles and knelt to pray.

Two candles? Carl looked to the reporter. "She lost her folks in a car accident a couple of years ago. Took it real hard. I guess if you had not made it, she would have blamed herself."

The past several hours, and all those years in which he agonized about his beautiful Elenna descended on him. He sank to his knees and covered his face and the bitterness flowed out of him. "I don't understand," he said. "I don't understand." He kept shaking his head to stop the tears.

They drove to Helen's apartment. She made a hot breakfast and Carl shaved and showered. Then Helen brought out a box of clothing. "My father's," she said. "They may fit you."

"Well, I thank you, Helen, but you should keep them for . . ."

"No, Mr. Cramer. It's time I let go. Time to let go."

Then they drove Carl to the bus depot and waited for the bus to Albuquerque. Helen took some money from her purse and put it in Carl's hands. "A loan," she insisted. Carl looked away. A man's tears were private.

They sat in silence.

Carl looked at Helen. She had large, sad eyes. It was almost like looking into eyes of long, long ago. "You know, Helen, I had a daughter. She would be about your age today."

She took his hand and smiled.

The bus came. "Let's not lose touch," Helen said.

As he boarded the bus, he looked back to her. "Her name was Elenna," he said.

Helen nodded and smiled.

He watched her standing at the curb as the bus pulled away. She grew smaller. Small enough to cradle in his arms.

FOR THE LOVE OF BONNIE

She was a beautiful, sweet, sheltered girl—the kind you married,
but I was not ready and able, so how not to stand in her way?
Fiction, but very close to the truth.

I met her at a community dance. She was standing in the corner of the hall looking very pretty but self-conscious and nervous as though she would have preferred to be somewhere else. I walked over and asked for a dance. She looked up at me, stood, and I took her hand and led her onto the floor.

There was a quality about her appearance that had me thinking of Mona Lisa. She had dark, curly, shoulder-length hair, and eyebrows and lashes that were full and perfectly formed and as dark as the hair on her head. Very pretty. Full lips and a cute nose that was a trifle large.

Usually talkative, I had difficulty starting a conversation. At last I blurted my name. "My name is Joe."

"Bonnie." That's all. Okay. And she would not look me in the eyes.

She danced guardedly as though measuring the exact, proper distance her body should be from mine. I felt like a masher every time we made contact when other dancers bumped into us.

She seemed not to be enjoying this, so we danced only once. I walked her to her seat, thanked her and melted into the crowd.

I did not see Bonnie the half-dozen times I returned to the dance hall. But I kept thinking about her. She must be a very sheltered girl to be so shy. She was not conceited, that's for sure. She was just not aware how beautiful she was, and that she had every reason to hold her head high and feel appreciated.

Then one evening I saw her at the dance again. Several men

DYING IS NO BIG DEAL

danced with her and seemed to have the same difficulty communicating as I had. When we made eye contact, I waved at her and she smiled and I went over.

"The music is too fast on this set. Can we wait for something slower?" The most words she had spoken since I knew her. We did dance a bit and it ended too soon for me. One thing for sure, I was not going to let her go.

I caught her actually smiling at one point as we talked. "I didn't know your smiling muscles worked," I said and was rewarded with a radiant smile. I was making progress. I asked if I could drive her home from the dance, and she nodded toward a pretty blond girl sitting nearby.

"I'm with my sister," she said. Apparently going home with someone who was not her date would not do. I asked for her phone number and was surprised when she gave it to me.

On our first date we went to a movie. I tried to put my arm around her but she smiled and said, "Let's just watch the movie, okay?" At this point I had decided enough was enough. This girl should have been a nun!

After the movie we stopped at Wally's for hamburgers and fries. I watched as she ate. This girl had a rare beauty. So how come I was so lucky to be with her?

"Why are you always looking at me that way?" she asked.

"Because you are a very beautiful girl. Don't you know that?" She was embarrassed.

We talked. I told her I was a student with about two years to go to graduation. She was a secretary and a graduate from business school. Italian. Had only a sister. She asked if I went to church. Did she? She said yes on Sundays and Holy Days and sometimes once or twice during the week. Like I said. This girl should have been a nun.

Afterwards we parked on a darkened street near her home. I put my arms around her and her hands came part way around me. So far so good. I decided to get bold and kissed her. Wow! Those full lips made my temperature soar. Then I let my hands roam.

"My God!" she shouted and leaned back against the seat. "Why are you guys always grabbing at a girl? Does it make you feel macho?" She spread her arms wide and shook her head. "Go ahead. Go ahead and help yourself."

Well, that took all the steam out of this adventure.

I can't remember much of what we said afterwards, although we did sit and talk for about an hour before I drove her home.

"You're really angry with me," I said.

"Disappointed, Joe. You seemed like such a nice guy." Then she leaned forward and kissed me and went inside.

She seemed surprised when I called for another date. "I didn't think you'd ever call me again," she said.

"I didn't think you would even talk to me. Do you want to go out?"

"Sure."

"And then we can make mad, passionate love," I joked.

She laughed.

We dated a couple of times a week. I liked her more and more, and we grew comfortable with each other. But ours was a controlled romance. Arms-around kissing was okay but hands off, otherwise. My respect for her grew.

Something else about Bonnie that I liked was her family. Her father, Anthony, was a short, pleasant man. Soft voice. Always smiling. And Bonnie's mother, Maria, was a stouter version of Bonnie with the same glow shining through.

I looked forward to being with them. Anthony was always cordial and offered homemade wine. They invited me to dinner and the pasta and Anthony's wine were memorable. Bonnie was always at my side serving. I ate with gusto, which they appreciated.

No doubt about it, I was in love with all of them. And Bonnie was precious. I found myself drinking in the sight of her.

"What?" she would ask when she caught me watching.

I just shook my head and sighed. I was head-over-heels in love with this beautiful girl.

What was it about her, exactly? She was gorgeous, but it was not the first time I dated beautiful girls. What Bonnie had was this pure, old-fashioned attitude I dreamed about meeting some day when I came back from the war. It boiled down to the word "wife." Oh my! Was I ready for that?

Thoughts of Bonnie interfered with my studies and even had me reconsidering my goals of a degree and building a career first. Wow! How could this happen so suddenly?

I told Bonnie my education and career plans, emphasizing how long it would take for me to become a wage earner. She did not volunteer comments. She watched me closely as I went into moments of silence, thinking about all this, and took my hand and held it tightly. She was aware.

I became part of Bonnie's family. I went to family gatherings and found her relatives a lot of fun, warm and friendly. I watched how Bonnie handled the little children. They flocked to her. And they all looked at me as though saying, "See how wonderful Bonnie is? So what are you waiting for?"

It was at a family picnic that I first saw Alfredo. It was a revelation! I watched Alfredo constantly looking at Bonnie and Bonnie's eyes kept seeking him out in the crowd. Even when Bonnie was talking to someone else, her eyes looked for Alfredo. And Alfredo peeked around people to see Bonnie. Hey! She never looked at me that way. My God! These two were in love, so why weren't they here together?

"Who is that handsome young fellow over there?" I asked Bonnie, pointing to Alfredo.

"Oh, that's Alfredo," she said, blushing.

"A relative?"

"Oh, no! He is a friend of my cousin, Flori."

"Have you known him long?"

"Yes, long," she whispered, acutely embarrassed.

An accordion appeared and everyone began singing and dancing. "Come on, Joe. Dance with me." I tried a few turns but this was a bit out of my league. I escorted Bonnie to sit with a group of her friends, excused myself and walked to the portable bar to get some refreshments. I found myself standing next to Alfredo.

"Hi, my name is Joe," I said.

"Alfredo," he said offering a firm, warm handshake. He barely looked at me. His eyes were following Bonnie and she was peeking through the crowd at him.

And so I watched them. They were very much alike. Both were shy. Very respectful. Nice people. I liked the guy but was feeling a bit jealous. So what should an honorable guy do?

"Alfredo, would you do me a favor?"

"If I can, Joe."

"I'm a terrible dancer, especially with this Italian music. I know Bonnie would love to dance and I want her to enjoy herself. Would you please ask her to dance with you?"

Alfredo was shocked. "But she is with you."

"That's all right. Do me a favor."

"Joe, she wouldn't dance with me. She is with you."

"Oh, come on. We'll ask her together."

He resisted but I took his arm, and we walked toward Bonnie who became increasingly uncomfortable as we approached.

"Bonnie, you know I can't handle this kind of dancing. I asked Alfredo to do me a favor to dance with you. Please."

"But . . ."

"Come on, Bonnie. Have some fun." I pushed them together.

So they danced and I watched. They didn't even know I existed anymore. The music changed but they danced on, looking at each other shyly and smiling. Alfredo held her gently and with great respect.

Bonnie's friends and relatives kept looking at me, watching my reaction to what was happening. I believe they all understood. These two were meant for each other.

After the dance and we were about to go home, I chatted with Alfredo.

"Isn't she wonderful?" I asked.

"Oh, yes. She is the most beautiful girl I ever knew."

"Don't be angry, but if you think so highly of her, why haven't you been dating her?" He was becoming angry now.

"It could never be, Joe," he whispered.

"Why not?"

"I am nothing. Just a car mechanic. She deserves more. You are going to college. You will be somebody some day."

After the picnic ended, we were standing together, saying our goodbyes. I could feel the power between them. There was a deep hurt in Alfredo's eyes, and a solemn, sad smile on Bonnie's face. We shook hands. When Bonnie extended her hand to Alfredo, he took it tenderly, and their goodbyes sounded like the end of the world.

I felt like a heel. I had no right being here. Somehow I had to find a way to bring these two lovebirds together. This would be real tough . . . on me.

I took Bonnie home and she hid her face from me. There were tears in her eyes. She gave me a brief hug and rushed into the house. A few times afterwards when I called, Bonnie's mother answered. Bonnie was not home. Cool, distant.

"Tell her that I called."

"I will."

The picnic scenes played over and over in my mind. I was jealous that someone had stolen my Bonnie's heart. My Bonnie? Was she ever really mine? I was holding back a commitment and had her waiting on me. I was unsure. That wasn't fair. Maybe it was fate that I saw how attracted Bonnie and Alfredo were to each other. These two danced their way into each other's hearts and I knew they were still dancing.

Well, I really messed this up! Bonnie would not talk to me, and I knew that Alfredo was not aware of this. What to do?

One day, at school, a couple of classmates and I discussed the situation. Stephanie, she was in my math class, and my friend, Bill Wismer, offered to help. No way would I let these two interfere, especially when they persisted with an audacious, corny plan. Stephanie wrote a perfumed note to Alfredo: "Please meet me at the dance this Saturday, at eight o'clock. Signed, Bonnie." And Bill Wismer wrote a note to Bonnie from Alfredo, same words, and added an authentic mechanic's touch—a smudge of auto grease on the envelope. They handed me the cards and I said I would think about it, but Stephanie yanked the cards from me and Bill mailed them before I could stop it.

A lot of nail biting followed. What if this happened? What if that happened? Stephanie, our surrogate Bonnie, sighed and insisted. "Don't worry. Love will take care of it."

Being away from Bonnie made a mess of my mind. Dozens of times I had to slap my hand off the phone to keep from calling her. What good would it do? Face it—what would be, would be. Time heals, they say. Very slowly.

Well, I completed my education and started a career in the accounting business, but beautiful Bonnie memories kept persisting. I had to know! I phoned Alfredo's house with no idea what I would say. His mother remembered me from the picnic.

"He doesn't live here anymore," she said. "He and Bonnie are married."

Okay. Okay. That's what I wanted. Right?

About five years after that picnic, I was shopping at the mall and I saw them. Bonnie was as beautiful as ever and Alfredo, proud and happy, held her hand and pushed a stroller in which sat a most beautiful baby girl.

I tried disappearing but Alfredo saw me and got hold of me. He was not angry. They were happy to see me. All smiles and glowing. I asked about the little one.

"Theresa," Bonnie said her name.

"Beautiful!" I would know that child was theirs no matter where I saw her. She possessed the beauty of both parents.

We talked briefly and as I was about to move on, Alfredo took my hand. "I want to thank you, Joe," he said, tears misting his eyes. Then Bonnie threw her arms around me, in front of all those people, standing on her toes, and kissed me full on the lips. The sweetest kiss I ever had. I quickly looked to see how Alfredo was reacting to his wife's enthusiastic kiss. He was smiling. I was smiling. So was Bonnie. My insides expanded to ten times the breadth of the mall.

I watched them walk away. They were chatting, holding hands, and with them was beautiful Theresa. Now that kind of love is rare. Something to remember . . . forever.

Goodbye . . . dearest Bonnie.

DYING IS NO BIG DEAL

A self-serving account executive uses people to elevate his position. This story came fast and won an international short story prize.

Mark Welker had abhorred and avoided violence all of his life. His world had been dispassionate, orderly, more or less comparable to the quiet printouts from the complex computer programs he developed.

He considered himself a fair and gentle man. His friends and family said he was too nice for his own good. Naïve, in fact. Well, they were right. And now, for the first time in his life, Mark felt he could actually kill someone. Specifically, Phil Ward, with whom he had worked as consultant for half a year to develop an intricate computer system for the Harcourt Corporation.

The system was in place and working beautifully. Even Phil Ward could handle it from here on. It was a tough, tough grind. He hardly saw his family through the day and night push. But Phil had dangled a big carrot. "Get this system working right, Mark, and you'll run the department. It'll be all yours."

Mark had been promised a vice presidency, an excellent salary, fringe benefits, company car, and stock options—the works. On the strength of these promises, Mark and Marie had scraped and borrowed all of the cash they could for a down payment on a new home. Their loan was approved, and they were to move in within a month.

This was to be the big day. The system worked. Bugs were ironed out. Now for the reward. Mr. Simmons's secretary met Mark at the door and said the president wanted to see him right away. You bet.

When Mr. Simmons spoke, Mark wondered if he was in the right room. Mr. Simmons said he was pleased with Mark's accomplishments. The company certainly would use his services again in the future. Phil Ward added his thanks and the meeting was over.

Outside, Mark grabbed Phil's arm. "You miserable . . . You double-crossed me."

"Don't get ticked at me, Mark. You heard what the boss said."

"You were in trouble, and I bailed you out, Phil. Then you knifed me in the back."

"Mark, I don't have time to discuss this. We're giving you a generous three months' bonus. And I'll draft you a strong letter of recommendation."

"You dirty son of a bitch."

"Watch it, Mark. I can get you more work in the future. You may need me for referrals."

"Works both ways, Phil. You'll never get another computer specialist to work with you. I'll see to that."

"You kidding? I've got dozens of prospects knocking at our door every month. You're good, but business is business."

Mark did not bother to clean out his desk. He had to get out. Instead of taking the elevator, he rushed down the stairs and out of the building onto Main Street. He passed a phone booth. It reminded him that he was to call Marie to give her the good news. God! How was he going to tell her?

The business section on Main Street was coming alive. Mark kept bumping into people rushing to their jobs.

Mark turned the corner off Main onto Sixth Street. Head down, hands in his pockets, he actually was talking to himself. He was so immersed in his own thoughts he did not quite connect what was suddenly going on in front of him. He saw a gun in the hand of a man hunched over the open window of a station wagon parked at the curb. There was a weird mask covering the gunman's face, and he was shouting to the wagon driver. "Hurry up. Give me your wallet. And the watch. Hurry, dammit."

A woman in the front seat of the wagon held a little girl on her lap, and the child was screaming. A little boy in the back seat was crying. Across the street, a red Pontiac four-door sedan, motor running, was aimed in the opposite direction of the wagon. Its driver also wore a mask and kept saying, "Hurry up. Get it over with."

A few passersby gaped then scurried away from the scene.

By then, Mark was within twenty feet of the gunman, who was too busy waving his gun to notice. Only seconds had elapsed since Mark turned the corner, but his mind had a slow-motion reaction as he already was dashing around the front of the wagon toward the gunman. The gunman cocked the gun and put it to the head of the wagon driver.

"No-oo-oo-oo!" Mark yelled.

The gunman, shocked by the intrusion, turned toward Mark, but he still aimed at the wagon driver. Mark hit the gunman's arm upward, and the gun went off, bullets breaking windows in the apartment building behind them. The wagon driver capitalized on the interruption, jammed the accelerator, and raced away.

The gunman shrugged Mark aside as if he were a toy and aimed at the departing wagon. Mark kicked the gunman's leg, and the shots went wild, knocking out store windows across Main Street. Then Mark threw both arms around the gunman's knees, and they wrestled, with the gun going off and bullets breaking windows and ricocheting off the pavement.

As they struggled, the mask came off the gunman's face. Mark stared into an ugly, square face that had a day's growth of beard and a broad scar across the bridge of the nose. The man's shaggy, gray-streaked hair seemed to stand on end. His attention and anger had focused on Mark, and he aimed at Mark's head.

"Well, so now you know what I look like. Too bad for you, hero."

Mark rolled aside and kicked up as the gun went off again. He heard the gunman yell. "Goddammit, I'm hit."

Mark looked up and saw the man holding his right leg. Blood seeped through the trousers and over his fingers. He aimed at Mark again and pulled the trigger. Nothing happened. That last shot had emptied the pistol.

"Come on, Vito," the driver in the Pontiac yelled.

"Shuddup, you stupid shit!" the gunman yelled back at the driver. Then he grabbed Mark by his hair, jerked him to his feet, and shoved him onto the floor of the back seat of the car. The man called Vito jumped on top of Mark and yelled, "Let's go after him!"

"Where? He's gone."

"There's only one place he's going, dummy. Let's go.

"The courthouse?"

"You talk too much. Take the expressway. If we can't catch up, maybe we can meet him there."

Then Vito looked at Mark. "Here," he said, handing him his necktie. "Put this around my leg before I bleed to death."

Mark fashioned a tourniquet with Vito's tie and ballpoint pen. From his position on the floor, he could see that they were speeding eastward on Eleven Mile Road. Then they turned north onto I-75. The car jerked into high speed. The driver zigzagged between lanes, braking, maneuvering, accelerating. He was good. Then he yelled, "There he is!"

"Pull alongside," Vito said. "And give me your gun. Mine's dry."

As Vito moved to the right side of the rear seat and rolled down the window, Mark eased up on his elbows. He could see the rear window of the station wagon come into view. Vito cocked the gun and aimed. "So long, sucker," he said.

Mark kicked upward. He felt his shoe sink into Vito's stomach. The shot never went off, but Vito reflexively swung the pistol in a short arc that caught Mark on his forehead. Then Vito resumed his aim. Mark reached over the back of the driver's seat, grabbed the driver's hair, and yanked. The car swerved wildly and Vito's gun went off. "Missed," Vito growled. "Damn!"

They heard the police siren and Vito yelled, "Let's get offa here." He hit Mark again with the gun, and Mark felt blood flow down his face.

They screeched onto an exit ramp off I-75. The siren became louder. Then shots were fired by pursuing police.

Vito opened the rear window wide and fired back. Bullets hit the Pontiac, and one passed through the rear seat inches above Mark's head and went through the driver's seat. He heard the driver grunt. "Vito. I'm hit."

"Keep moving!" Vito yelled, and continued firing. Mark heard a tire blow, a screeching of tires, and a crash. "Got him." Vito laughed. But the Pontiac slowed, went onto the shoulder, and slid to a stop in the ditch alongside the road.

"Come on," Vito said, aiming the gun at Mark. They climbed out of the car. Vito looked at the driver. "Dead." He reached into the driver's pockets, taking identification and a handful of bullets from the dead man's jacket. He turned toward Mark. "Come on." He grabbed a handful of Mark's hair and pulled him into the ditch. A car was approaching.

"Lie down," Vito told Mark. He hid his gun behind his back and walked out of the ditch. A tan Dodge sedan pulled alongside. An older couple was inside.

"Are you all right?" the old man asked.

"Just fine, mister," Vito said, aiming the gun at the man. "Now just get outta the car peacefullike and tell your old lady to get out, too. Hurry up."

They got out. "You." Vito pointed at Mark. "Drive."

They stayed clear of main roads. Vito directed Mark to turn onto a narrow gravel road north of Rochester. They drove slowly as Vito scanned both sides of the road, looking over the homes which were set far back off the road. Then he told Mark to pull into a narrow, tree-lined drive. This was a secluded lot. About a hundred yards away from the road was an old ranch house. A beat-up Dodge pickup truck was parked inside a rickety garage.

"Pull in behind the garage," Vito ordered.

They got out and walked toward the house. Vito pounded on the side door and waited. He knocked again, then tried the door. It was locked. He broke the window with his pistol, reached in, and unlocked the door. He pushed Mark inside. They walked from room to room. Nobody was home.

"Good," Vito said. He entered the kitchen, opened cupboards, and found a jar of instant coffee. "Boil some water and make us some coffee."

Vito sat in a kitchen chair and groaned. "Damn. It hurts." He rubbed his wounded leg. His pants were caked with blood and there was fresh blood flowing. Vito picked up a kitchen knife, slashed open his right pant leg, and examined the wound. "Went right through," he said. Then he looked at Mark. "Don't make any difference. I'm a dead man, thanks to you."

Mark made the coffee and placed a cup in front of Vito, who motioned for Mark to sit in the chair opposite him at the table.

"Do you know this Wilson?" he asked.

"What?"

"The guy in the wagon I was holding up. Do you know him?"

"No."

"Then what in the hell did you stick your neck out for? Now look at all the trouble you got yourself into."

Mark did not answer.

"I asked you, dammit. Why did you butt in?"

"The man's wife and kids were in the car."

"I wasn't going to hurt the broad or the kids."

Mark looked away and sipped his coffee.

"Oh, I get it," Vito said. "You did it because of the broad and the kids. If there were no kids in the car, would you do what you did anyway?"

Mark shrugged.

"You married?"

"Yes."

"Any kids?"

Mark nodded.

"How many?"

"Two."

"How old are they?"

"Three and six."

"Boys or girls?"

"What's the difference?"

"I asked you, boys or girls?"

"One of each."

"Which one's three?"

"The daughter."

"Ain't that nice? You stick your big nose in somebody else's business, and now the kids ain't never gonna see their poppa again. How does it feel now to be a fucking hero?"

Vito took another gulp of coffee. "Give me your wallet," he said.

"What for?"

Vito cocked his pistol and aimed it. "Give me your fucking wallet."

Mark reached into his back pocket and tossed his wallet at Vito. "Here. You won't get rich on what's in there."

Vito did not take out the money. He looked through the wallet compartments until he found the pictures of Mary and the children. "Nice looking broad. How's she in bed?" He laughed.

Mark stood up, moving toward Vito.

"Sit down, hero. Don't fuck with me or I'll shoot your balls off and let you go. Then what good would you ever be?"

Vito looked at the pictures again. "The little girl is cute. The boy looks like you." He watched Mark and, when he did not respond, Vito tossed back the wallet.

They studied each other, drinking their coffee.

If the opportunity came, could Mark subdue this man? He was hurt, but he was powerfully built. Short. Maybe five feet six inches. Big in the shoulders. His body was wide and muscular.

Vito looked at Mark. "What the fuck you looking at?"

Vito's head was square, the same as his body. Large head. Thick black hair, graying in spots and needing a trim. The hair curled along his neck and the sideburns bushed out. Clumps of hair grew out of his ears. He had a large nose which appeared to have been broken many times, and it had that wide scar across the bridge.

"I said, what the fuck you looking at?"

"You. You're an animal. Do you actually enjoy doing what you do?"

"It's a living." Vito shrugged.

"Killing people is a living? How many have you murdered?"

"I stopped counting after thirty."

"Thirty people? You killed thirty people?"

Vito shrugged and yawned. "I don't remember what number you will be."

"Why not kill me right now? What are you waiting for?"

"I'm gonna need a driver. You're it." Vito laughed. "How does it make you feel, hero, knowing that you don't have much time left?"

Mark shrugged. "Hell, I'm worth more dead than alive—today, anyway."

The coffee relaxed Mark's muscles. He almost forgot Vito was there. Well, the day started off lousy, and things just kept getting worse. He had three strikes on him already. Instead of a promotion, he got fired. Strike one. Without the promotion, they would lose the house. Strike two. And then this cold-blooded killer came along. Strike three.

"I said, what do you mean 'strike three?'" Vito asked.

Mark did not realize he had said it aloud. He might as well explain to Vito. A lot of good that would do. But, to his surprise, Vito listened and appeared to grow increasingly angry at what Phil Ward had done to him.

"This guy at Harcourt who fucked you out of the job—can he handle what you set up?"

Mark shrugged. "Sure. I worked out all the bugs. He can take it from there."

"I don't know nothing about these computers. But I know about guys like this prick who screwed you. Well, maybe somebody will give him the business."

"Nah. There's nobody there. No competition. That's the way Phil Ward wants it. He's Mr. Big now."

"What if something happened to him, and he wasn't there? Who does the job then?"

Mark became aware of how Vito's mind worked. He knew what Vito would do if he were in his place. Mark's eyes widened as he understood what Vito was getting at. Vito smiled, pointed his gun at an imaginary Phil Ward, and said, "Bang!"

They finished their coffee. Vito looked for a phone. "I gotta call to find out about *my* third strike."

He dialed and Mark heard him say, "Jake? I ran into some trouble." He listened and his expression grew grave. "He showed up, huh? That's what I was going to tell you. Things got screwed up. Uh-huh. So Carlo's really not pissed off at me. He says everything's cool. Uh-huh. He wants me to know it's all right. The lawyer, huh? He's got things all worked out. What's that? You want to know where I'm at. Sure you do. Fuck you, Jake." He slammed down the phone.

Vito looked at Mark. "You think you got trouble, hero? You don't know what trouble is until you have it with Carlo. You're gonna die fast. Me? When they get their hands on me, I'll wish I was never born."

"I don't get it," Mark said. "Who's after you? I guess it's not the cops you're worrying about."

"Shuddup," Vito growled.

"Hey, I ought to know what's going on." Mark became angry. "You're waving your gun at me and telling me I'm going to die. For what? All I tried to do was keep somebody from getting killed."

"Sure. We're both going down," Vito said. "So, I'll tell you what you being a fucking hero has done to me."

Vito began pacing the kitchen again. "This Wilson was shooting off his mouth. One of his buddies's got knocked off because he got Carlo mad. Personal mad. This friend of Wilson's had evidence about Carlo's business."

"What kind of business?"

"What the hell's the difference. It was business. Anyway, Carlo could have put out a contract and let somebody else do the dirty work. But not this time. Carlo wanted to see the guy die. He did the guy in himself, and that stupid fucking Wilson saw it happen."

"Wilson called the cops?"

"The FBI. We told Wilson he'd get killed if he didn't shuddup. Threatened his wife and kids. The dummy didn't know when he was well off."

"I heard your driver mention the courthouse. Was Wilson testifying?"

"This morning. And I got stuck with making sure he didn't get there, because I goofed on Wilson's contract before. Gave the contract to one of my men to get Wilson, and the dumb bastard knocked off the wrong guy."

"You mean some other guy got killed, too?"

"Any asshole should have done it easy. A truck loaded with cement. Out of control. Hits the station wagon and bye-bye Wilson. Only the dumb-shit driver hit the wrong station wagon. Poor sucker in the wagon never knew what hit him or why."

"I want to throw up," Mark said.

"Hey. You win some; you lose some. Law of averages. Now you, you're something else. You must have ten lives. I shot at you and shot at you, and I kept getting kicked. I hate your guts, you know, but I gotta hand it to you. You're a slippery, tricky son of a bitch."

Vito got up and limped toward the rear window. "I might as well blow my brains out right here. That would be quick and easy."

"Why don't you just call the police and turn yourself in? You might even get immunity as a witness against this Carlo and go free."

"You gotta be kidding. There ain't no place safe in the world. They'd get me in no time. Besides, I'm not going to fink on my own people."

Mark laughed. "Oh, so you're going to be a hero now. Finking is against your code. Go down in honor."

"Shuddup, you son of a bitch. You got me into this mess. I ain't ever messed up before you stuck your goddamn nose in my business. So shuddup or I'll blow you away right now."

Vito paced the kitchen and kept watching the clock. He smoked up the last of his cigarettes. He limped badly and blood that had seeped into his shoe left tracks on the floor. All the while, he kept looking at Mark as though deciding what to do with him.

Mark did not care anymore. He was exhausted. Drained. He

thought of Marie and the little ones. What would they do without him?

Concern for Marie and the children turned Mark's thoughts toward escaping. There was some hope. He was still alive. Vito could have killed him hours ago. But if he was going to be shot by this crazy killer, why not rush him and try to overcome him? Vito was getting careless, walking close to Mark as he paced back and forth. He would jump Vito, get the gun and, even if he could just knock him down and run out the door, he might make it.

Mark's heart beat faster. His face felt hot. He placed his fingers on the edge of the table and planned to push it into Vito as he turned to walk away from him. Now!

Mark shoved the table and then followed it as if he were pushing a cart. It connected with Vito's rump. Surprised, Vito tried to turn around, but the pressure of the table against him kept him stumbling forward. Vito fell, and the hand holding the gun hit the floor. Mark yanked the gun free. Vito twisted around catlike and grabbed Mark by the throat and squeezed.

Mark pressed the gun against Vito's ear. "Stop, Vito, or I'll shoot. I mean it."

Vito's grip relaxed, his hand fell away, and he rolled over on his back, gasping for air. "You son of a bitch. Ain't you ever gonna get off my fucking case?"

Mark removed his necktie and tied Vito's hands behind his back. Vito lay on his stomach and groaned.

"Now, let's take a look at that leg. I don't want you to die until the cops come. Then I don't give a shit."

"Hey, what happened to that nice guy who didn't like to see people die?" Vito laughed.

"You're not people. You're an animal. Let me see that leg."

Mark loosened the necktie which served as a tourniquet and tore the pant leg upward, exposing the entire leg. He removed Vito's shoe and blood-soaked sock. Then he went to the bathroom and looked into the medicine cabinet. He returned with gauze, antiseptic, a towel, and a wet washcloth. He cleansed the wound

and poured antiseptic over it, causing Vito to wince. Then Mark
bandaged the leg.

"Well, Vito, you're lucky. The bullet went through. The
bleeding has slowed. Now I'm going to call the police and bring
an ambulance, and they'll fix you up."

"Don't call the fucking fuzz. Soon as they get your call, some
of Carlo's boys will know and beat them to me. Why not just plug
me? You can turn me in dead or alive and be the big hero. Go on,
shoot me. Come on, shoot, you fucking wimp."

"I couldn't kill anybody. Not even a snake like you."

"Cut the crap. You're killing me no matter what you do. If
Carlo's boys get to me, the police won't ever find me. Not a clue.
Whether you turn me in or shoot me, you're finishing me anyway.
Pull the fucking trigger."

Mark picked up the phone, explained to the police what had
happened, and gave directions where to find them.

He had just put down the phone when a chair hit his head
and Vito landed on Mark's back. When he turned around, Vito
kicked him in the head and the lights went out.

The police found Mark unconscious. When he revived, he heard
the walkie-talkies and saw the flashing red lights of the police cars
swarming outside. They carried Mark to the ambulance.

The police had the Dodge sedan in the driveway and were
inspecting it for clues. The old Dodge pickup was gone. Mark
tried to tell them that Vito must have driven off in the pickup, but
he realized his jaw was broken. Anyway, he could not keep his eyes
open.

They took Mark to the Crittenden Hospital in Rochester.
When he awoke, he found that his jaw had been wired and there
were many people in his room. Marie was there and, outside his
room, the police and several reporters clamored to talk to him.

When they saw he was conscious, the police went in. They
were after Vito. Mark answered their questions by writing on a
pad they had provided. Obviously, they had not captured Vito.

Off and on, as he would wake, he watched TV newscasts. There was a constant flow of bulletins about the aborted hit and about the hero in the hospital who saved the witness's life.

Early on the third day, Marie brought the newspapers. She pointed to the story Mark had been looking for. There was a picture of Vito lying flat on his back alongside the Dodge pickup. He still wore the same clothing. The split pants showed the bandaged leg Mark had worked on. Vito's body was sprawled with his arms outstretched, as though welcoming someone. There were numerous bloody bullet holes over his body. "Gunman Dies in Shoot-out!" the headline read.

> *Vito Micelli, gunman, allegedly a hit man for Don Carlo, an underworld figure on trial for murder, died as he had lived, violently. Police, alerted to a holdup committed by Micelli, closed in after a high-speed chase through heavily trafficked Woodward suburbs. The chase ended in Pontiac on Opdycke Road near the Pontiac Silverdome when Micelli's pickup truck rammed into a utility pole.*
>
> *Police Chief Edwin Marshall of Pontiac said Micelli was wanted for questioning on numerous crimes. 'But this time we had him dead-to-rights. He shot this guy during the holdup, an executive of Harcourt Corporation. The victim was dead on arrival at the hospital.'*
>
> *Officer Wilfred Lutz, one of the pursuing policemen, said 'The guy was weird. He got out of his truck and fired a couple of shots at us. When we surrounded him, he just broke and made a run toward our car. We had no choice but shoot. He was laughing. Firing and coming at us and laughing. It was him or us. He really got shot up.'*

That afternoon, Harcourt Corporation President Jim Simmons came to visit. "Mark, we're all proud of you. It took a lot of courage to do what you did."

Mark could not respond because his mouth was wired shut. The pad and pencil lay alongside his bed, but he did not plan to use them.

Simmons smiled but fidgeted nervously. There was something else on his mind. Before he left, he said, "When you are strong enough and on your feet, Mark, we want you to return to your job with us. Don't worry about it now. Just get well. The project will be all yours. There's a substantial bonus in it for you, too."

Simmons turned and headed for the door. Mark cleared his throat and, as Simmons turned to him, Mark waved his hands, indicating he had a message for him. He wrote only two words on the pad. They were words Mark never used—words more appropriate to Vito's vocabulary.

Simmons stooped to see better. He read the words. He looked into Mark's eyes and nodded his understanding. Then he shrugged and walked off.

Mark lay back and sighed. It would have been easy to take Simmons's offer. He was out of work now. They had to pay for that house. It was the principle of the thing. He had to do what he felt was right. Then he laughed. What did doing what was right get him so far?

Those were days to remember. They began in despair and the kind of anger Mark had not been capable of. And he had experienced fear as never before. He had tested his courage. After what he had been through, nothing, absolutely nothing that lay ahead would be insurmountable.

For a moment, his mind flashed over those terrifying hours with Vito. He smiled as he realized that even in the heart of the most miserable, amoral human he had ever met, there was a last, kind thought for someone else.

"Wherever you are, Vito, thanks anyway. You no-good son of a bitch."

GLOW

I saw this very attractive, petite girl in a used-book store. Couldn't get her out of my mind. I imagined becoming a hero on a white horse rescuing her.

"We buy and sell books," said the sign above the rickety building that might at one time have been a garage. It sat opposite the Village library near the county park of the peaceful, suburban community.

It was the first time in years that he had shopped this bookstore. The clerk was a pert, slender blond dressed in snug black slacks and a vest over a high-necked pearl gray blouse. She would be needle-thin were it not for an obvious bulge of pregnancy. Her hair was pulled back into a bun emphasizing crescent earrings that danced wildly as she moved about.

"May I help you?"

His mind was totally occupied with her pleasant face. She looked up at him, waiting. Could not be more than five feet tall.

"Looking for some Tony Hillerman paperbacks," he said.

"Oh, his used books don't last long. Have a few new ones in that rack over there. Twenty percent discount on new paperbacks."

He followed her to a revolving bookrack. She was tiny, like a young teenager although he had decided she must be at least twenty-five years old, give or take a year. He stood beside her not looking at the books but into her eyes. Like looking into an open sky. Thin, beautiful face. Such a pretty thing!

"Uh, thank you," he said, taking the book offered to him. As he observed no ring on her finger, she quickly withdrew her hand.

He watched as she moved about helping customers, obviously enjoying her work—smiling and talking a lot and occasionally looking his way, catching him gawking.

He chose the book she had handed him and placed it on the

counter.

"We get a lot of used books each week. I could call you when some Hillermans come in. Do you have any titles in mind?"

She was waiting for an answer. He was trying to remember. The last time here he had seen an impersonal middle-aged woman tending the store. Former teacher he had learned.

"Are you the new owner?" he asked.

"Oh, no. I'm just filling in for my aunt who just got married and went off to Scotland with her husband."

"Scotland?"

"Yes," she giggled. "We don't expect her back very soon." She handed him his change and inserted a marker in the book. "My name is Cynthia. What's yours?"

She held open a notebook with spaces for names and phone numbers and book titles requested.

"Charles. Charles Carson."

She wrote his name along with a note, "Hillerman titles." Then she looked up, waiting for a phone number.

Leaving the store he nearly collided with a woman carrying a large paper bag filled with books. He held open the door for the woman and hoped Cynthia did not see him bumbling.

"God!" he said, shaking his head, embarrassed for acting like a clod. The vision of her face kept popping into mind throughout the day.

The store was ten miles from his apartment but he returned often. He bought books he did not need and realized that he had better read them because Cynthia often asked how he liked a particular book he had bought. She seemed more pleasant each time he returned.

Don Wheeler, Charles' roommate, looking at the accumulation of books in the living room, asked, "Hey, Chuck. You starting a library?"

Charles was grateful for an opportunity to talk about Cynthia. "Don, you've got to come along and see this creature. The most exquisite face and so sweet and unaffected. She takes my breath away."

"But didn't you say she's pregnant?" Don groaned. "For gosh sakes, Chuck, she's already hooked-up with someone. Walk away before you're confronted by her jealous poppa-to-be."

"There's no ring on her finger."

"Chuck, walk away from it. There are a lot of beautiful, wonderful, single girls around. Why this one?"

"For gosh sakes, I'm not having a relationship with her. Just like to watch her. And that voice!"

With each visit to the store Charles observed something new about her that increased his interest. She had a habit of touching when she talked. A hand on his arm when directing him to books. Or her hand pressed on his as she shared an earnest idea about a story or author. And there was that thank you handshake when he paid for his purchases. Her hand was soft and warm but the handshake was firm and lingered. And she kept looking into his eyes as though trying to peek into his mind.

His Cynthia complication was temporarily relieved when a film script he had written for his agency for an industrial firm was approved. He was to go on location to Houston with the camera crew for several weeks. During free moments as filming progressed, Cynthia's blue eyes and pretty face kept intruding, and he thought about her and heard that infectious catch in her voice, and remembered the growing bulge of motherhood.

"Who's Cynthia?" one of the grips who leaned over Charles' shoulder asked, pointing to the doodles on Charles' pad. "Cynthia" was scrawled all over it.

Back in town he convinced himself he needed a particular book. Not because he wanted to see Cynthia, just to get that book.

She smiled as he came in. "Were you on vacation?"

"On business," he said, pleased that she had noticed his absence.

He had to know more about her. Somehow he must talk to her, away from the store.

"Cynthia?"

She looked up at him with such a warm, friendly smile. "Yes?"

What to say? Words jumbled and swam away.

"Uh, Cynthia. Would you have dinner with me some evening? To talk about books."

Startled a moment, she smiled. "Oh, thank you for asking, Charles. But . . . how about coffee at the donut shop across the street? Marlis, my helper, should be here soon to relieve me."

Main Street was heavily trafficked. He tried to hold her elbow to assist her across but she took his arm and hurried with quick, short steps.

She ordered Diet Coke. "None of that fattening stuff for me," she laughed, patting her belly.

What to start talking about? He shook his head, frustrated.

"Are you uncomfortable being seen with an expectant mother, Charles?" she teased.

"Oh, no!"

Then he could not shut up. He told her about the large family he came from in Ohio. Four sisters and three brothers. "Seemed that at least one of my sisters was expecting most of the time."

He cringed. Now why did he have to mention pregnant sisters? She smiled.

He learned that she worked at the store while attending the local university, majoring in music. "Piano is my specialty," she said, floating her hands across an imaginary keyboard. Thin, graceful fingers. Then she self-consciously placed her hand over that bare ring finger.

On their way back to the store they walked slowly and said little. He held onto her arm. "May I see you again?"

"For lunch?" she asked.

"No. A date. That okay with you?"

She hesitated. "How about a movie? Sunday. Only day the store is closed."

She lived with two students in an upstairs flat of an old frame house around the corner from the store. After their first date it was easier for him to see her again. He took her to a play at the university. They dined at a cozy restaurant where there was music and dancing. They tried a turn on the floor but she led him back to their table after just one dance. "Thanks, Charles, but either I need longer arms to hold onto you or more space down here."

They walked in the campus park. Conversation was limited to his listening. Her animated facial expressions and constant use of her hands kept him captivated.

"What are you laughing at?" she asked. "Did I tell a joke?"

"No. I just enjoy watching your perpetual motion. Wish I had a cameraman here to get it all on film."

"You *are* making fun of me."

"No. You're just fun to watch."

"Yes, you are making fun of me," she said, grabbing hold of his ribs, tickling him. He put his arms around her, a natural motion, but it caused them to stop and look at each other and feel uncomfortable. She took his arm and they resumed walking. "Tell me, Charles. What's a nice, handsome young man like you wasting time dating a momma-to-be?"

"You don't like my company?"

"Sure, but look around you. All the pretty, unattached girls. There's no future for you in dating me."

"Is that a brush-off?"

"No." She squeezed his arm. "I enjoy being with you but it's . . ."

"What?"

"Well, look at me." She puffed up her cheeks and made wide motions with her hands. "A blimp. With a problem."

"But I think you're beautiful."

"Beautiful? Charles, a pregnant woman is not beautiful. She waddles like a duck. Is so conscious of her big belly and everybody is looking at her and snickering."

"It's a pity women are not aware how special they are when they're pregnant, and the respect they get from everyone."

"Come on, Charles."

"There's sort of a glow about them."

"Charlie, you're weird."

"No. There is a softness of their features. A gentleness. It's even in their eyes, the way they look at you."

She put fingers in her ears and shook her head. "You're just trying to make me feel good about it. You don't have to do that. Look at me!"

And she did an exaggerated waddle, puffed her cheeks and crossed her eyes.

How could he justify his feelings with words? Coming from a large, close family, he had a deep respect for children. News of a new life was cause for rejoicing. He remembered watching his sisters and sisters-in-law being showered with affection during pregnancies. He was conscious that a tiny life in them would soon arrive and another child would be running around the house, jumping on his lap as he tried to relax, demanding he tell stories or insisting he take part in their exhausting games. Melodramatic? Sure he was. How could he not be.

"Pregnant girls don't look sexy," Cynthia said. "What do you say about that, Charlie?"

"There is a time for sexy and a time for little miracles," he said.

She studied him, wide-eyed, then burst into tears.

He put his arms around her.

At her flat, she looked up at him strangely, then led him inside.

"My dear Charles, you are such a darling. In this day and age you are something special. Thank God that you have such a loving family. I hope that some day you find a girl worthy of your respect. But, dear, you are becoming much too close to me, and I fear that it is because you feel obligated to rescue a damsel in distress. I have no pressure about this. It was a brief, beautiful moment. Even now I can't figure out what happened, but it did and no regrets, honestly. Can you understand?"

He said he did, but did not.

"It was a tender moment. We were close but not in love. Then, when he went away to school, I learned about the baby."

"Shouldn't you tell him?"

"I may never see him again. He had such grand dreams about his future. I'm sure that if he knew about the baby he would probably fumble around trying to do the honorable thing. But I would not want to forever have him feel that he married me out of necessity. What kind of life would that be to build on, huh?"

He frowned.

"Early in my pregnancy, friends talked to me about options. There are no options for me. I'm going to have this child."

"The child should have a father."

"Of course it should."

"Well . . . well . . . how about me? No secret how I feel about you."

"Charles, you are a sweetheart. But don't feel you should be involved. Let's just be friends. Unless it is uncomfortable for you to be seen with a huge, pregnant friend," she giggled.

"What about your folks?"

"They understand and support me all the way."

"Strange family," he said putting his arms around her. She began sobbing and melted in his arms.

From that evening on, Charles and Cynthia felt more comfortable with each other. She allowed him to go with her to the doctor and to her Lamaze meetings. They were *together*.

In her eighth month Cynthia became extremely moody and restless and weepy. Occasionally, she was a bit cross, which she apologized for later.

Seeing a depressed Charles, roommate Don asked, "Problems in the motherhood romance?"

"She's holding me off, Don. I can only get so close and . . ."

"What do you mean by close?"

"I want to marry her but she keeps shushing me up and changes the subject. I'm really in love with her."

"Charlie, my friend, she is trying to do you a favor."

"So what if she is carrying someone else's child. It will be her child. No problem for me there."

"Ah, Charles, the knight on a white horse, banners flying, rescuing the damsel."

"Truth is, I just can't go on living without her."

"You've told her all that?"

"Of course. I don't know what else to do."

Don thought a moment. "How about this. Talk is cheap. How about a ring?"

"What?"

"Give her an engagement ring. Nothing more convincing about commitment than putting a ring on the lady's finger."

Charles leaped to his feet and reached for the phone directory. "I'm stupid. Why didn't I think of that?"

By noon, next day, Charles had purchased a ring and sped to the bookstore. He rehearsed how he would do it. He hoped the store would be crowded. Then he would talk loudly to draw an audience. On bended knee he would tell her he loved her and wanted her to be his wife. There would be a lot of snickering as this guy proposed to a very pregnant woman. But how could she refuse? Yes. Just like in the movies.

There were no parking spaces near the store. Good! That meant lots of people inside. He double-parked. To heck with a parking citation. Marlis was behind the counter.

"Where is Cynthia?"

"She's not here, Charles."

"Where?"

Marlis shrugged. "She didn't say. Most likely gone to her parents' home."

Her folks lived in Stanford, sixty miles away. He got there in less than an hour. Cynthia's mother opened the door. He sagged into the chair they offered him.

They could not tell him where she was. Mother said, "Cynthia told us about you, Charles."

He stayed for dinner. When it was time to go, he paused to look at pictures on the mantle. Cynthia, age two, cute, blond, curly-haired child with mischief written on her face. Age ten, a pious Cynthia for her First Holy Communion picture. Cynthia as a cheerleader. And Cynthia, the athlete, her baseball cap askew and arms around fellow players.

"She was a beautiful child," he said.

"Beautiful! Then, and always. The love of our lives, Charles."

There were no pictures of other children.

"Was she your only child?" he asked.

"Yes. We could not have children of our own." Tear-filled eyes looked up at him.

No children of their own?

Mother took an envelope out of her apron pocket and handed it to Charles. "Read it later, Charles. Please!"

In the car he unsealed the envelope. Inside was a pink, flower-patterned card. A slight scent of cologne. Her handwriting was as beautiful as everything else about her.

"Dear Charles. Thanks. Love, Cynthia." A lipstick kiss.

He remembered her pictures. A life filled with love and joy. Someone's love given to her parents.

He would wait. He would see her again. The scented card went into his shirt pocket, near his heart.

THE LAST JUMP

What could happen to an "always-play-it-safe" individual who is diagnosed to be terminal?

Doctor Cohen was explaining in more detail but Harvey abruptly stood and brushed past him and walked out of the office. In his car in the parking lot, Harvey blinked, trying to comprehend what was told to him. He kept shaking his head, not having it all sink in.

He started his car and waited, trying to decide what to do and where to go. Certainly he was not ready to go home to tell Esther. He drove onto the northbound I-75, nearly being brushed off the road by a semi.

Good old, careful Harvey Hough! Two years into retirement and now *this*. Could there be a mistake? Of course not! Doctor Cohen showed the x-rays pointing to a large mass in the stomach area and extending near the liver and kidneys.

"Cancer?" Harvey asked. Doctor Cohen looked away then back at Harvey and shrugged.

"Can we do something about it?"

Cohen shrugged again. If he shrugged one more time Harvey decided he would kick him! Cohen explained. First, the pain would become increasingly severe. They could do something about the pain. Later, there would be a loss of bodily functions. That meant going to the hospital. Then, another shrug from Cohen.

"Don't tell my wife," Harvey had said. "Let me handle it."

Now Harvey maneuvered his car to the center lane of the expressway. How could this have happened? He was so careful. Medical exam every year. Watched his weight and cholesterol level. Skipped the ice cream and butter and homogenized milk. Watched his red meat intake. He did not smoke. Did not drink. He should live to be a hundred! Then came the stomach pains. Nothing he could not handle but Esther insisted he should see Doctor Cohen. And the doctor sent him to the x-ray center.

Suddenly Harvey was aware of his driving speed. Over seventy! Whoa! Watch out, he cautioned himself. Then he laughed. Force of habit. The family joke was "Don't let dad drive. Take a week before we get there." Well, Harvey adhered to the letter of the law. Even when highway speeds were raised to sixty-five Harvey drove the more comfortable fifty-five. And his passengers had to buckle-up before Harvey started up. "It's the law," he insisted. He remembered Fred Schneider, a co-worker, teasing. "For gosh sakes, Harvey. You can't live forever."

Harvey moved slowly off the road to the shoulder and turned off the engine. He slumped over the steering wheel. Fred Schneider's teasing words, again. "You can't live forever, Harvey. You can't live forever."

Well, time to go home and get himself organized. He would not tell Esther, but he would get financial details and beneficiary information together for her, to make it easier for her once he was gone.

At home, Harvey examined his life insurance policies. There was one from his company, another personal policy for fifty thousand, and an old GI policy for ten thousand. Esther would be adequately provided for. There were notes about his pension benefits and dividend income from stocks and mutual funds. All this he put into an envelope on which he wrote, "Open in the event of my death." He slipped this beneath his shirts in the dresser.

Now he was ready for whatever.

He felt no pain for days. Was this the calm before the end? To keep his mind occupied he went for rides in the country. As he was passing a large meadow near the county airport, he saw several parachutes open high overhead. He pulled off the road to watch. There were four of them. Colorful chutes, slowly descending with tiny figures attached, maneuvering toward an area in the open field where a van waited. The chutists touched ground and gathered up their chutes. He could hear their excited chatter as they loaded their gear into the van.

Wow! If only he had the courage to do something as exciting as that. Harvey followed the van to the airport. He stood beside his car and watched. Their leader, probably the trainer, was directing them, joking with the men. There was one woman and three men.

The trainer saw Harvey and approached. "Hi! Interested in jumping?" The man was short, muscular, tough-looking, but friendly. "I'm Biff Walker. I train these daredevils. Biff Walker's Skydiving School."

"How does it feel?" Harvey asked.

"To jump? Exciting as hell. Really makes you feel alive. You see the whole world below you like you never dreamed it could be. You interested?"

"Nah! I'm too old for that stuff."

"You kidding? Here, let me show you something." Harvey followed Biff into the office. Biff picked up a clipping from a California newspaper which was enclosed in a cellophane cover. "Here's a guy, 75 years old, who jumps every week. He started when he was 65."

Skydiving? Old stick-in-the-mud Harvey Hough? The idea was ludicrous. But what better way to go. What did he have to lose now? For the first time in his life he could test his courage, feel the excitement and be daring. The worst that could happen would be he could get killed. Hah!

Esther had no idea where Harvey spent so much time during the week. He came home flushed, excited. Thank God! For a while she was worried about him. When she asked where he was going he told her he had joined a club. What kind of club? Sort of a geographic study group. They studied the terrain of the county. Very interesting activities.

Biff Walker started Harvey jumping off a low platform at the airport to learn how to land properly. Then Harvey and three other beginners went up for their first jump. There were three static jumps where the chutes were attached to a static line in the plane so the chutes opened automatically as the jumper left the plane.

The first jumps were a bit frightening, but once out of the plane and descending, Harvey felt so exhilarated that he shouted with joy. It was so peaceful up there, and quiet, just the drone of the plane from which they jumped. The land below was a checkerboard of colors with miniature houses and buildings. Automobiles barely crawled on the roads and people were the size of ants. Made one feel God-like.

The free-fall jumps were something else. Now Harvey had to pull the ripcord. If the main chute did not open there was the back-up chute. You could not afford to freeze-up or pass out. The jumper had control, when to pull the cord. Who could tell if . . . .

The training plan called for three five-second free-fall jumps. Then ten-second free-falls. Ultimately, sixty-seconds.

"Remember," Biff cautioned. "You're dropping at one hundred and twenty miles per hour. In ten seconds you drop twelve hundred feet! Watch your time. Don't get too carried away with the scenery."

It was during the ten-second free-fall that Harvey began to visualize that last jump. He would fall and fall and fall and go out like a man, by golly. If only Fred Schneider knew. If he were up there with Harvey, he would mess in his pants. And Harvey would kid him, "Hey, Fred. You can't live forever. Right?"

Harvey almost forgot about his health problem. There were only a few stabs of pain, but nothing serious. One day, however, he doubled up in pain. Deep thrusts in his stomach shortly after he had eaten took away his breath. Esther had picked up the phone to call the doctor. "No," Harvey said. "It'll go away. Put down the phone, Esther. I'll see the doc in the morning, all right?"

Well, it had come. Harvey watched Esther's concern and felt sorry for her. Maybe it was not fair not to tell her. But why should he worry her? What could she do about it?

Well, this was the day to do it. Harvey hugged Esther and kissed her gently then went to his car. Esther stood at the door and waved to him. Almost as though she knew.

Biff Walker announced, "Today we do the sixty-second free-fall. The optimum jump. You'll be pros. Then we'll get into more exotic jumps—group jumps, free-fall maneuvers. Anything and everything. How about that?"

They all cheered.

The sixty-second free-fall. The perfect last jump for Harvey.

"Why so quiet, Harv?" Biff asked.

"Who me?" Harvey shrugged. As he shrugged it reminded him of Doctor Cohen's shrugging habit. Boy, what would the doc think if he knew what Harvey was going to do today.

"Come on, Harvey. If you have any feelings about this, we can put you off until another time. Pick your own time. Do a ten-second free-fall instead. No hurry."

"No, I've been looking forward to this jump, Biff. I'm ready.

At the clinic, Doctor Cohen's nurse, Dorothy O'Connell, interrupted the doctor while he was attending a patient. "Not now, Dorothy," he said. "I'll be through in a minute."

"Doctor, this has to do with some urgent information about x-rays from the x-ray center."

Cohen excused himself and followed Dorothy to his office and picked up the phone.

Doctor Sylvester at the x-ray center explained there was a mix-up in x-rays sent to Cohen. They had a client whose name was H. Houghton who it was believed had a stomach ulcer, according to x-rays delivered to Houghton's physician. But Mr. Houghton collapsed and another series of tests showed there was widespread stomach cancer. The x-rays for Doctor Cohen's patient, Harvey Hough, because of the similarity of patient names, got mixed up. Actually, Harvey Hough's x-rays showed only a stomach ulcer.

"Oh, my God!" Cohen groaned.

Doctor Cohen called Harvey's home and Esther answered. "Harvey's not here," she said. "Is anything wrong?"

"I must talk to Harvey. Where is he?"

"He went out and I'm worried about him."

"Why? What's the matter?"

"Well, he kissed me and held onto me a long time before leaving the house. He hasn't done that in years. And I found an envelope in his dresser which looks like his will or something. What's going on?"

"I'll be right over," Cohen said and dashed out of his office.

Biff Walker had two other jumpers in the plane making the sixty-second free-fall with Harvey. As they circled the drop area, Biff watched the expression on Harvey's face.

"Harvey, are you okay?"

"Sure. I'm fine."

"You can change your mind. Try the jump some other time."

"No, today's the day."

At the Hough's residence, Doctor Cohen mentioned an x-ray mix-up.

"My God!" Esther said. "No wonder Harvey seemed so pre-occupied and tense. But he never complained."

"He never told you anything?"

"No. What was he supposed to tell me?"

"Do you know where he went?" Cohen persisted.

"No, but there is a brochure on his dresser. Probably the club he belongs to."

The brochure advertised Biff Walker's Skydiving and Hand Gliding School.

"Oh, no!" Cohen groaned. "Come on with me."

Cohen sped to the airport. The girl at the office pointed to the sky where a Cessna 182 circled higher and higher above the field. "Biff's taken some jumpers up. Should be back soon."

In the plane the pilot signaled to Biff. Biff tapped Harvey on the shoulder. "Okay, Harv. Remember. Sixty seconds and pull the cord. Don't exceed sixty seconds. Harv?"

"Got it, Biff. Listen, I want to thank you for being so patient with me. I know I wasn't the quickest to learn."

"You were great, Harvey," Biff said, watching Harvey somewhat reluctantly move toward the door.

The plane surged upward as Harvey jumped, just as a call from the tower came for Biff. The pilot handed the headphones to Biff. "They say it's urgent."

Biff listened. His eyes widened, and he looked down at Harvey's body hurtling earthward. Twenty seconds. Thirty seconds. Biff watched as Harvey did some twists and turns, unscheduled maneuvers. "Oh, God!" Biff groaned. "Come on, Harvey. Don't do it. Don't do it."

Below, Doctor Cohen and Esther watched a jumper's body plummet. Esther began screaming. "His chute won't open. His chute's not opening."

"Pull the cord, Harvey," Cohen hissed.

In the plane Biff counted the seconds. Sixty seconds. Harvey, darn it, pull the cord.

"Pull the cord," Cohen shouted. "Please pull the cord."

Biff shook his head. That's it. Too late. It's too late.

All eyes were on Harvey's body tumbling now, perilously close to earth. Then, suddenly, the chute blossomed open. Harvey's body jerked upward and disappeared below a rise of land. They jumped into the van and sped to the landing site.

Harvey lay on the ground, motionless. The chute billowed in the wind. Several members leaped out of the van to collect the chute which was now dragging Harvey's body on the ground.

"He's alive. He's breathing," one jumper said.

Doctor Cohen and Esther stood over Harvey. He opened his eyes, surprised to see them. They helped him to his feet. He was groggy but apparently able to move unhurt.

"You pulled the cord," Doctor Cohen said.

Harvey was puzzled. Then he understood. The doctor knew what Harvey had planned to do.

Harvey nodded. He looked up at the sky and blinked. A smile. A broad, incredible smile spread on his weary face. "It was so beautiful. Up there it's so . . . like . . . another world. I wanted one more jump."

"Harvey," Cohen said. "I showed you the wrong x-ray. You're all right."

Harvey's smile vanished, replaced with a mean frightening scowl. When Cohen shrugged, Harvey planted his feet solidly on the ground. He was going to do it. He would kick him. Cohen moved backwards, frightened.

Then Harvey laughed. He laughed so hard his sides hurt him. He put his arms around Esther and Cohen as they helped him into the van.

THE EGO STING

A club tennis player in a tournament tends to blame others for her poor performance. She needed a comeuppance.

I'm the head pro at the Suncrest Tennis Club. Our members are really nice people. They enjoy the game and display good sportsmanship. But I guess I aged some on this job when Priscilla Fraser came along.

When Priscilla joined our club, she knocked us right off our feet with her beauty. She had a regal quality about her: An exquisite figure, a Grace Kelly-type face, and rich, blond hair. The closer you came to her the better she looked. Until she started talking. She could not open her mouth without insulting someone. She was the most unfeeling and inconsiderate person I had ever met. And she flaunted her beauty until you felt like gagging.

Priscilla's husband, Derek, was just the opposite of her. He was as handsome as she was pretty, but a quiet person who could use some vanity. He probably contributed to Priscilla's ego problem because he laughed at her cutting remarks, considering them a kind of sophisticated sense of humor. For his sake we tried extra-hard to put up with his wife.

Priscilla had alienated so many people we had a difficult time matching her up with someone to play with. She believed herself to be a good player, but the truth is she was terrible. She was uncoordinated. She crowded balls so that many of her attempted return shots tipped her racket and went skittering off to the other courts. And she was slow, so many easy shots just went past her. Her serves were adequate thanks to the persistence of one of our pros who worked daily with her. But Priscilla was oblivious of her playing weaknesses. When teams she was on lost a match, she could be overheard saying, "Well, I can't do it all by myself."

We figured it was just a matter of time before Priscilla would go too far. Most players agreed that it was time her ego should be taken down a peg or two.

We were just starting up our early-season women's doubles matches when Priscilla chose the wrong person to insult. We were waiting on her to do her warm-up stretches. She grasped the net post and bent and wiggled and tilted her pelvis and got a lot of attention and whistles from spectators. When she finally appeared ready, she took her position on the court and gave a haughty nod to let us know we could commence. Then she held up her hand to halt the game and called over the match manager and pointed to the relatively-new member, Kitty Eilers, who was to be Priscilla's partner.

"Who picked her to play with me?" Priscilla asked.

"Why? What's wrong with Kitty?" the manager asked.

"I've seen her play. I don't want her. Get someone else."

The timing could not have been worse. Team match-ups had been posted for days. If she had any objections, Priscilla had ample time to say so. The players groaned but Kitty was a good sport. She walked off the court and another player was selected. It occurred to me that Priscilla was not concerned about Kitty's playing skill. She was more concerned about the attention Kitty would take away from her. Kitty was a stunning redhead with a figure equal to Priscilla's, and she looked a lot sexier, too, without even trying.

So Kitty played the match with someone else and fumed. There was no doubt that she would even the score with Priscilla somehow. Kitty had a mean streak in her that would not permit a slap to go unslapped.

Word got around about Priscilla's insult. Speculation grew as to how Kitty would serve up Priscilla's comeuppance. The players encouraged Kitty to do so by repeatedly bringing up the matter.

Several weeks passed without a response from Kitty. We wondered if maybe the storm between these two would pass, especially because Kitty had practically stopped coming to the club.

Early one morning as I was on my way to the club, I thought I saw Kitty's red hair and trim figure on the public courts near the civic center. She was volleying with a skinny, blond, pony-tailed girl. They were really going at it! I pulled into the parking area and walked over. Yeah, it was Kitty all right, working up a heckuva sweat and looking very excited.

"So, this is where you've been hanging out," I said.

She concentrated on playing. "Hi, Tony," she said.

"What are you playing with this skinny kid out here for? Bring her to the club."

"Not yet."

I watched the action. The kid lacked finesse. Her movements were herky-jerky, and she hit the ball at awkward angles, but rarely failed to get the ball back. And she was swift. Those skinny legs of hers were in perpetual motion: A skip, a jump, springing up and down on the toes, flashing around the court, forward, backward, side-to-side. Wow! Her serves were strictly set-toss-and-pow! Nothing fancy, but with good velocity and most first serves were right in there. This kid could be developed into a quality player. I guessed that's what Kitty was doing—smoothing out the kid's rough spots.

"Relative of yours?" I asked Kitty.

"Don't I wish," she said. "Her name's Jenny Malone. Isn't she something? No matter where I hit the ball, and I've tried every trick I know, she hits the ball back. Just wears you down."

"Yeah," I said. "I noticed. Why not bring her in? We can work with her."

"I've got something else in mind. And you better keep quiet about this for now, okay?"

"Sure," I said. I'm not stupid. I could see a sting in the making.

Kitty brought Jenny in a couple of days later and introduced her to me. I liked the kid right away. She looked around at the beautiful courts, the terrace with its tables and juice bar, and the members moving about so elegantly dressed in designer outfits and swinging expensive rackets. If Kitty wanted to have Jenny appear out of place here, she surely accomplished that. Jenny had on worn, cut-off shorts and T-shirt and beat-up tennis shoes. She clutched an old wooden racket that, if it was a car, would probably have a couple of hundred thousand miles clocked on it.

"Well, Jenny," I said. "Welcome to the club."

"Thank you, Mr. Marino."

"Please call me Tony," I said. She smiled. I knew it would always be Mr. Marino.

When Priscilla arrived and seated herself at a table near the courts, Kitty took Jenny down and they started volleying, but casually, so as not to let out of the bag how good this kid was. Priscilla watched and laughed. She jerked her thumb at Kitty and Jenny and said something that brought tittering from a few spectators.

Making sure that Priscilla had seen the brief display of Jenny's playing, Kitty motioned for Jenny to follow her and they sat at a table next to Priscilla.

Priscilla was amused. "I see the quality of this club is going downhill," she said.

Kitty clenched her fists but kept her cool. "Good morning, Priscilla," she said. "I have a friend here I'd like you to meet. This is Jenny Malone. Jenny, meet Mrs. Priscilla Fraser."

Jenny stood and put out her hand. Priscilla regarded her coolly and looked away. A crowd gathered around. There were a lot more people here than usual. I suspect Kitty told a few friends about Jenny and they were in on the sting.

Unsuspecting, Priscilla helped things along. "Playing with kids lately, Kitty?" she teased.

The spectators moved closer, leaning to catch every word.

"Well, this kid's pretty good," Kitty said.

"Oh, really? About your speed, huh?" Priscilla laughed.

Snickers and a few guffaws from the spectators.

"No, she's really good. Could beat me *or you*," Kitty was setting the hook.

"No doubt she could give you a good run," Priscilla sniffed.

"Oh, I think she could give you a good game. In fact, she could beat you," Kitty's voice was firming.

"Huh!" Priscilla scoffed.

"If betting were allowed, I'd lay odds she could run you right off the courts."

Priscilla laughed, looked Jenny over and shook her head.

"Would you like to try her?" Kitty said.

"Don't waste my time. *You* play her. She's more your speed." Priscilla finished her juice, stood, and beckoned to her playing partner to follow her to the courts.

"What's the matter, Priscilla? You afraid? Is the great know-it-all Priscilla Fraser afraid to take on an inexperienced kid? You really don't play well and you know it."

Jenny turned her face away and tried to move from the confrontation. I'm sure the kid had no idea she was being used. Kitty held onto Jenny's shoulder and urged the spectators to pressure Priscilla into playing a match. The words between these two grew more heated until I was afraid they might get physical so I stepped in.

"What's going on?" I asked.

"Priscilla just insulted Jenny's ability. If she's so damned good why won't she take Jenny out there and show us." Kitty was shouting now.

More voices encouraged a match and Priscilla became angrier and embarrassed. Then she wheeled around, her face red and she spat out the words. "All right, big mouth. You've been a pain to me ever since you came to the club. Let's get this over with. I'll play your ragamuffin and when I beat her, I want you and the kid gone. Permanently!"

"Fine," Kitty said. "But it goes both ways. You lose and *you're* gone, permanently."

"Fat chance," Priscilla said. "Best out of three sets. Get us an umpire."

Chairs scraped and there was a scuffling of feet as spectators scrambled for a good view. I volunteered to umpire. Jenny won the toss for first serve.

Kitty provided last minute encouragement to Jenny. "Now, Jenny, we are playing a match. It's no different than what you've been playing on the public courts. Priscilla tires easily so keep her deep and run her from side to side. And she's slow, as you will see. Her worst shot is the backhand, so work on that. The way you play you'll have her cross-eyed, bowlegged tired in no time."

Priscilla was making Jenny wait, trying to intimidate her. She went into her warm-up stretches—twisting, stretching, waggling, taking her time. Then she looked across at Jenny and lifted her arms upward in exasperation. "What am I doing here playing this crummy little kid?" She said that loudly enough for Jenny to hear. Then she faced Jenny and made an imperious gesture for her to serve.

The first volleys went to at least a dozen exchanges. Priscilla hit the ball as hard as she could and deep, and Jenny returned the balls easily—to Priscilla's forehand, then to her backhand, moving Priscilla back and forth, back and forth. And Jenny showed her snappy two-handed backhand. Priscilla's bored expression turned to one of interest and puzzlement.

The kid may have appeared to be a pushover at first, but now she matched Priscilla stroke for stroke and moved the ball around well. Then Priscilla lost patience and hit the ball deep then ran in to the net trying to intimidate the kid. Jenny coolly hit a neat passing shot and all Priscilla could do was watch it sail by. Fifteen love, favor Jenny.

The second series of volleys, like the first, went back and forth, both playing a waiting game for the other player to make a mistake. Priscilla's brow furrowed. She hit the ball deep then followed with an excellent drop shot. Jenny sprinted toward the net and reached the ball easily. Priscilla, in mid-court, groaned as Jenny just tipped the ball over the net and scored the point. Thirty love, favor Jenny.

Priscilla scratched out a point here and there but the games went to Jenny. Two love, then three love. The kid had Priscilla talking to herself. She made astonishing shots. There were "oohhhs" and ahhs" from spectators when Jenny reached deep lob shots with ease and hit the ball backwards from impossible angles. Priscilla stared at the kid, shocked, and shook her head.

When the set went to four love, favor Jenny, Priscilla developed a tantrum. She tossed her racket into the air and kicked balls that she missed. Then the score went to five love. Kitty and her friends stamped their feet and clapped and cheered. "Sweep. Sweep. Sweep." I stopped the game and admonished them about sportsmanship.

In the sixth game Priscilla was pressing and tiring. She double-faulted twice to love thirty. Then she blew herself right out of the set by recklessly lashing hard shots that Jenny let go out.

With the first set concluded, a sweep for Jenny, Priscilla turned her back to the spectators. I could hear her sob with frustration. Jenny was looking at her and waiting to resume play but Priscilla stalled. Jenny walked over to talk to me.

"Mr. Marino," she said, "I don't feel good."

"You sick, honey?"

"No," she said. Her eyes turned toward Priscilla who continued standing off court, back toward the spectators and in deep thought. "It's not right what we're doing."

"Honey, we can't quit now. You'll lose the match. It's the rules, you know."

She nodded. "It's her face," Jenny said. "Look at her face."

Yeah, I could see it. The great Priscilla Fraser looked like a beaten, old woman. Wilted. Subdued. I hated to see that although she had it coming. "Jenny," I reminded her. "You have to get back there and play."

Jenny walked to her position. She looked up at Kitty who was in the front row, stamping her feet and clapping her hands along with her friends. They came to see Priscilla beaten and shamed. Jenny paused then turned toward me, and I nodded for her to get going.

And so we began the second set.

Suddenly Jenny made consecutive bad plays. She slammed a ball into the net. Her lobs went out. She failed to reach balls that were easily within her range. She scored a couple of points but lost the first two games. Now Priscilla took on new life. Her confidence returned as did her arrogance. She began strutting and laughed when Jenny faulted on a few easy return shots.

You know how tennis goes. You're hot and nothing you do can go wrong. Then, all of a sudden, like the wind coming from a different direction, you lose the touch. That's the way it appeared as Jenny kept losing points. But I wasn't buying that. She was carrying Priscilla! She felt sorry for her. Well, she had better not go on too long with this; otherwise, it could affect her real game. Never tamper with the rhythm of your game.

The set went to three love, favor Priscilla, and then we were into the fourth game with Priscilla getting the first point. That's when Priscilla called Jenny to the net. She believed she had the kid beaten and was gloating. I heard her say some demeaning things to the kid to beat her down. Jenny's eyes opened wide. She blinked, holding back tears. I hit the ceiling and reprimanded Priscilla, and she just laughed at me. Her ego was so inflated she could not appreciate that the kid was trying to lighten the beating Priscilla had been taking.

Jenny's blue eyes filled with tears, and you could see the gentleness slowly melt from her face. She went back to her position far back in the court. I could hear her sob. When she turned around, besides tears on her face, there was a look of hate that didn't belong on a kid this young.

Now Jenny played with a vengeance. She hit the balls with vicious strokes. She could not wait to return shots and slammed the balls back. The balls went past Priscilla. They ricocheted off her racket. One hard shot hit Priscilla in the midsection and I heard her groan.

Priscilla's three game advantage disappeared. The set went three and three. Then four to three and five games to three, favor Jenny.

The next game—and it would be the last if Jenny won it— went to forty love, favor Jenny. Jenny called time and came to discuss a point with me. Was there any way, she wanted to know, that we could stop this match with neither Priscilla nor Kitty being a loser? I just interpreted the rules. If Jenny walked, Priscilla would win by default even though she was far behind in games. There had been situations, I explained, where an injury halted a game until it could be determined if there should be a default or if the game might be rescheduled. It was tricky business. Did Priscilla know these rules? Jenny wanted to know. Sure. She knew the rules. That's when Jenny went to the net to talk to Priscilla. There was no ego left in Priscilla. She held down her head and listened. She nodded. And they went to their respective positions. Jenny needed one last point. She served a light tap that no one, even a six-year-old, could miss. Priscilla moved to the ball and hit it to Jenny's forehand. Jenny ran toward the ball then seemed to trip and she fell. She sat on the court holding her left ankle. I rushed to her. It appeared she could not stand.

I leaned over her. "Jenny. Are you hurt bad?"

She shook her head but looked toward Priscilla. Priscilla nodded and went to the end of her court, picked up her racket cover, put her racket in it and walked off.

"Mrs. Fraser," I called after her. "We're not finished here."

Priscilla opened the gate, walked up the stairs and went into the locker room.

Jenny stood and thanked me. I couldn't help myself. I hugged her. "Sweetheart, that was an excellent match," I said. She thanked me and walked away.

Kitty ran up and called after her. "Jenny. Jenny. Where are you going?"

"Kitty," I said. "She won't come back."

We watched Jenny, her ponytail swinging as she walked briskly toward the exit.

"You know," I said. "That's one fine kid you had there, Kitty. I hope you are satisfied with what you did."

We heard a loud slam as Jenny shut the door of the club behind her.

BYE-BYE, BABY

Going to bed one night the idea struck me: How would I handle a break-in?

He heard glass breaking. It came from the kitchen. Yes, he was sure of it.

He struggled out of bed and reached for the bed stand and his fingers felt for the drawer and opened it. The gun was there.

God! Someone was in his house. They were going to rob him. Maybe kill him! His heart was pounding and the pressure on his chest hurt and there was a ringing in his ears.

He took out the gun and crept to the hallway next to the kitchen. He stopped, straining to hear. Yes, there was someone in the kitchen. He heard them whispering.

He tried steadying his hand by holding onto the gun with both hands. He moved slowly to the doorway of the kitchen and peeked.

There were two of them! He could make them out silhouetted against the rear doorwall at the entrance to the family room. They seemed to be trying to make up their minds. It was too dark to see if they had weapons.

He tried to control the trembling and breathing, praying that the gun would not slip out of his hands and that his heart would not seize from fear.

He turned his head toward the front entrance, only a few feet away. He could reach the door and run outside and yell for help before the burglars could get to him. He could do that. But then, he thought, that wasn't right. They had broken into his home. If he ran now he would never forgive himself. No, that wouldn't be right.

He took a deep breath, quietly. He had to do something while they were close together.

"Let's go," he heard one of them whisper. So it was now or never, the old man thought. They had paused to size-up the house, and now they moved slowly around the table next to the doorwall. The old man had moved into the kitchen and slipped beside the refrigerator where he had some protection in case they shot at him. He gripped the pistol, let his other hand slide along the wall toward the light switch. He turned on the light and yelled so loud that he scared himself. "Put up your hands!"

The sudden light shocked them. They jerked up their hands and something in the hand of one of them went flying against the wall and fell to the floor.

"Keep your hands up. If you so much as move, I'll blow your brains out."

One of them had his back towards him while the other faced him. The one facing him was a boy.

"You," the old man yelled to the other one. "Turn around with both your hands up."

The other one turned toward him. It was a girl! A head shorter than the boy. She was trembling and begging. "Please don't shoot, mister. Don't shoot us, please." Her eyes were wide and crazy-like. Lips trembling.

Bullshit! He thought. They'd get what was coming to them. They broke into his house. They broke the law. The safety was off. He would shoot the boy, first. Right in the middle. Then the girl.

He slowly squeezed the trigger, watching the boy's eyes. But he loosened his grip on the trigger. He couldn't bring himself to shoot.

"Mister," the girl pleaded. "Have a heart. Look!" She undid her coat and he saw she wore a maternity dress and the big bulge showed she was far-along pregnant.

"Jesus Christ!" the old man groaned.

Then she cried and slowly slipped to the floor. The boy reached for her.

"No you don't!" the old man shouted. "Keep your hands up. I mean it."

The girl moaned and put her hands to her belly and gasped. "Oh, Timmy. Timmy, it hurts."

"God, mister! Please. She's in trouble. Can't I please help her?"

When the old man hesitated, the boy took off his coat and knelt beside her.

"Honey. Honey. Are you alright?"

"I knew we shouldn't do it. I knew we shouldn't."

The old man moved closer and kept the gun aimed.

"Timmy. Timmy." The girl gasped and was shaking and groaning. "I think it's coming. Oh, God! The baby's coming."

The boy turned to him. "Mister. For Christ's sake. Can't you help me? Call an ambulance. She's having the baby."

The old man watched them. The girl turned her head side to side crying out in pain. The phone was on the counter next to the stove. He moved to it, placed the gun on the counter and fumbled with the dial. He could not see the numbers clearly without his glasses. He put his head back to look at the dial.

Then he heard the girl's voice. "Okay, sweetheart. You can put down the phone. She had a nickel-plated pistol aimed at his heart. His eyes darted toward his gun, but he'd never reach it before she'd get off a shot.

The boy moved toward him, picked up the old man's gun and whipped it across his face. "Okay, you old fart. Get *your* hands up now and hurry or I'll put a shot into that fat gut of yours."

The old man felt blood running down his face from where he had been hit. He heard the girl laughing. "Old grandpas. They're easy."

Then she showed the old man her profile and lifted the hood of her maternity dress. The pregnant look was a pillow strapped to her belly. "Insurance," she said. "When somebody gets the drop on us. Works every time."

They tied him to a kitchen chair with a necktie from his bedroom and stuffed a dirty washrag into his mouth. Then they went through the house, and he could hear them rummaging through the bedroom dresser drawers and heard things being scattered on the floor.

"Bingo!" he heard the young man say. "Look at this."

They had found the jewelry box. Where his wife's wedding and engagement rings and jewelry were. And the money. He should have taken the money to the bank.

"Oh-h-h!" he heard the girl say. "Must be four or five hundred here. And isn't that a beautiful pearl necklace?"

The old man had bought Lucie that necklace as a wedding present. It was her favorite piece. He tugged on the binding on his wrists so the silky fabric would slip loose.

They returned to the kitchen holding a couple of bulging pillowcases.

"How you doing, pops?" the girl asked. She removed the gag.

The old man glared. "Take everything but, please, leave my wife's rings and necklace. I'll give you more money when I can get to the bank. Please! Those are all I have to remember her."

"Hah!" the girl shrieked. "Stupid, shit! We'll get a bundle for this stuff. And maybe we'll come back some day and get more of your money."

"Come on, Jan," the young man said. "Let's get the hell out of here."

"Wait a minute," she said. "Hey, pops. Got anything in the frig to drink? A pregnant gal gets awful thirsty." She nodded to the boy to look in the frig.

The boy opened the frig and took out two cans of Strohs and popped the lids and handed one to her.

She sat down in the chair opposite the old man and took a big sip.

The old man had difficulty breathing. He gasped, drawing in deep breaths.

The girl moved close to him and grasped him by the hair and pulled back his head. "Boy! You were one tough old fart," she said. "But you couldn't shoot a couple of nice kids like us. Could you?"

"No," he said. "But I should have."

"Then you saw little old me, big and pregnant, and you didn't have the heart, huh? Well, you should've done it when you had the chance, stupid old man."

The old man looked at her and shook his head. "I pity the children you ever have."

She slapped him hard across the face. He could feel the coagulated blood break and fresh blood trickle down his face.

The old man groaned and shook his head and put his head down on his chest.

"Whattsa matter, pop? You having a heart attack?"

He looked up, face contorted in pain. "Pills. Get me my pills. In the medicine cabinet in the bathroom. Please!"

She laughed. "What for? You kick the bucket, and we don't have to worry about you blabbing to the cops."

"If I die, and you get caught, it'll be more than burglary you'll pay for."

"Then maybe we ought to just pop you off before we leave."

The old man saw that the boy looked concerned and went to the bathroom. He heard him rummaging through the medicine cabinet.

The girl went to the frig for another beer. The old man wriggled his fingers and felt the tie fabric loosen more. He stopped when she came back to the chair and sat down in front of him.

The boy returned with the pills. "These the ones?" he asked.

The old man looked and nodded. He groaned and put his head down then far back and moaned. "The pain! Goddamit it hurts!"

The boy tossed the pills to the girl and asked. "How many?"

"Two," the old man said. "Two. And please, hurry!"

The girl asked, "What happens if you take more than two? Say, six or seven or ten? Hey!" She looked at the boy. "How about that for an idea? Get me some water, Tim." She opened the pill bottle and shook out a handful of pills. She had placed her gun on the table next to the beer. The old man thought he might be able to reach it if he could free his hand.

The girl grabbed his hair and yanked back his head. "Open your mouth. Open it."

The pain forced him to open his mouth, and she dumped the pills into his mouth then poured in the water and held his nose.

Struggling, he now freed his right arm and then spit the water and pills into her face.

"Damn!" she yelled and pulled back, wiping her face.

The boy was standing beside her watching her react. The old man reached for the girl's gun and aimed it at the boy and pulled the trigger. Nothing happened. The safety was on.

The boy, suddenly aware, reached for his gun tucked inside his belt. This time the safety was off and the old man aimed at the boy and shot him. He saw the blood appear in the middle of the boy's chest. A look of disbelief on the boy's face faded and his eyes went blank and he fell.

"You son-of-a-bitch," the girl yelled and dove for the gun. She fell against him, and he pushed the gun deep into the pillow.

He was looking right into her eyes. Her face was so close to him he felt her breath on his face.

"Please don't shoot, old man. Let me go and I'll give back your wife's things."

She slid down a bit to her knees and leaned sideways. He saw her left hand creep toward the gun on the floor near where the boy lay.

"Please, mister. Gimme a break."

He pulled the trigger. She shuddered and shook her head and he pulled the trigger again. She kept shaking her head and looking at him as she slipped off him onto the floor.

THE FISH WHO LOVED
OLD GRANDAD

*Most fishermen have a favorite story to tell. This one is a fantasy
of two bumbling fishermen trying to prove themselves by catching
an awesome fish.*

Marty and I have a reputation of being lousy fishermen and
tellers of tall tales. When other fishermen come in with full stringers,
we come in with excuses like—the wind was coming from the
wrong direction, or it was the wrong day of the month, or the fish
weren't biting because it rained last night, or we went out too late
in the day.

So when we told our wives that we were taking off a week to
try our luck fishing in Michigan's Upper Peninsula, we got the old
yuk-yuks that the only thing we'd catch up there would be a cold.

Well, this time we were going to come home loaded,
guaranteed, Marty insisted. He bought a beat-up, crude map for
fifty dollars from a guy who worked with us at the Chrysler Sterling
plant. It gave directions to an uncharted lake in the Upper Peninsula
that had the biggest freshwater fish you ever saw.

"It's worth fifty dollars," Marty insisted. "The guy lived in the
Upper Peninsula all his life, and he said there's practically nobody
there. Water's so clear and pure you could drink it. Fish so hungry
they practically took a bare hook. Right here," Marty pointed to
an area circled on the map north of Manistique, Michigan, in the
Hiawatha National Forest.

So that's where we were going. We got on the I-75 so early
that even the birds weren't awake yet. We crossed the Mackinac
Bridge at sunrise. The view was spectacular, but Marty told me to

stop being poetic about it and to punch the accelerator. Off the bridge we took US-2 out of St. Ignace and arrived at Manistique tired and hungry. We stopped for some food. "No fish, though," Marty insisted. "We're going to be eating plenty of that from now on."

When we turned north on H13 in the Hiawatha Forest and tried to locate the place scribbled on our fifty-dollar map, things got confusing. What were we looking for? Some familiar road sign? No. The map showed just an "x" where to turn off, somewhere about twenty miles up H13 to an unnamed road. Oh, yes. Right after we see a huge fallen birch tree. Mighty fuzzy directions!

Finally, Marty said, "Turn right here."

"There's no sign about a lake here, Marty."

"I'm sure this is the way."

So I turned. There was room on this dirt road for two cars to start with but gradually it got narrower, then abruptly it was just a path in the woods. With no room to turn around in to go back, so we had to keep going. The path veered to the right with water puddles hiding big bumps. This path ended at another path giving us a choice of going right or left.

"Turn right," Marty said. His guess was as good as mine now so I turned. Then he pointed. "Over there!"

It was a rickety sign leaning against a big beech tree. "Ma Finch's Sunshine Cabins."

A turn to the left and we came to a clearing and followed an arrow pointing to a row of eight cabins. These were log and mortar cabins, built a long time ago and not maintained much.

Nobody around, so we walked into a vacant cabin. It had a stone fireplace, a wood cook stove, a sink, but the hand pump was outside. Lights were gas-filament lanterns. Out the rear window I saw the outhouses set back about fifty feet into the woods.

I was about to tell Marty to forget it when he grabbed my arm and pointed out the window. "Lookit that lake!"

We walked onto a wobbly dock and gazed upon the prettiest lake we'd ever seen. Wide, blue, rolling water dotted with five or six little islands. Far beyond the lake appeared to open up to yet another lake. Seemed like no end to it.

"More fish in there than you'll ever see anywhere. Big fish. All kinds." The speaker was a tough-looking old gal with a few front teeth showing. "I'm Ma Finch. Cabins rent at one hundred fifty per week, including boat. That one's yours."

She could be anywhere from seventy to a hundred years old. Hair looked like she had just got up. She wore beat-up men's pants and an old flannel shirt. I smelled a whiff of booze on her breath.

The boat she pointed to was an old wooden job alongside several others that gently banged into the dock. Dozens of aluminum strips, painted over, appeared to hold it all together. There was practically as much water inside the boat as outside.

"Rained heavy last night," Ma said, catching me looking at the water-filled boat. "Well, yes or no? I ain't got all day."

"Just a minute," Marty said. At that, Ma stalked off spitting and grumbling.

"It's a flea bag of a place, Ed," Marty said. But as he looked from the cabins toward the lake, his face lit up. "But I'd sleep on the floor for a chance to try my luck here. And with such cruddy accommodations, why would anyone stay here if the fishing wasn't great?"

About this time a guy came rowing toward the dock, groaning and puffing but with a smile that told us he had some luck out there. He tied up and, without saying a word, hauled up a stringer with five big, I mean BIG, bass. Wow!

We rushed to Ma's cabin and gave her our money.

"One more thing," Ma said. "No motors. You row or you don't go. I don't want you stinking up my lake." At that she thrust a couple of chewed-up oars at us and vanished.

She wasn't cheap about bait. There was a live box with dip net and a sign, "Free, but don't hog it." We bailed out our boat and loaded up. Marty jammed our cooler with beer. We scooped up some bait and took off.

We didn't figure on much luck so late in the morning, but we got a couple of scrappy bass, anyway, both over a couple of pounds. "Hey. Our wives ought to see this," Marty held up the stringer.

We were way ahead of our usual fishing luck already, so we just leaned back, relaxed and sucked on our beers.

Man! It was a beautiful day. Lake was an artist's dream. Trees all around grew right to the shore. Big birch leaned toward the water. Mammoth pines, oak, maple, and ash. A fresh breeze gently drifted us toward a little inlet off the north side of one of the islands, just out of sight of Ma's dock. I looked down and saw that the water was so clear you could see almost every grain of sand and pebble at the bottom.

"My God!" Marty jabbed me and pointed. "Lookit there!" I followed his long arm aimed just aft of us in the lily pads. Partially hidden beneath the pads was a gigantic fish. A pike! It was as big around as me, almost, and nearly the length of an oar. Its pike markings were magnified by the clear, rippling water. "A pike. A whale!"

We tried to stay cool. Fresh baiting our lines, we cast gently as possible to either side of the pads, slowly reeling in. We let our bait wriggle nearly under the pike's nose and paused to let the minnow do its frantic dance, trying to escape those mean pike teeth. Nothing seemed to work.

We tried our entire arsenal of lures but the pike just stayed there watching us. Then he disappeared.

"You saw him, didn't you, Ed?" Marty wanted assurance that this wasn't just his imagination. I nodded. "It wasn't the beer, then." Marty shook his head. "We actually saw a monster pike. Biggest darn fish I ever saw."

We saw him, all right. But he wasn't there anymore. We probed around the pads hoping to get another look. He was gone. We rowed back, stunned.

Next morning we met Rufus. Actually, we overslept. All that excitement our first day took a lot out of us. But Rufus made enough noise to wake a hibernating bear.

He was piling firewood on our back porch. When I poked my head out I saw this tall, spindly stick of a guy stacking wood out of an ancient wheelbarrow. "Brought you some wood," he said. "I'm Rufus. Everybody calls me Rufe."

The name fit. A backwoods type. Lumberjack shirt. Woolen stocking cap on a top-shaped head. Small, beady eyes. He grinned and spat tobacco juice out of his toothless mouth. "Five dollars," he said. "I'll put some ice in your box later. Five dollars," he said, again.

"I'll get you later," I said. But he wasn't leaving so I went for my wallet.

"You always deliver this early?"

"It's not early," he said. "It's almost six o'clock."

He stuffed the five dollars into his pocket and scuffed off with his wobbly wheelbarrow. Six o'clock! Hey, we had no time to waste. "Get up, Marty. Let's get the heck out there."

We rowed straight for the spot where we saw the big pike. No sign of him. We baited and waited. I managed to haul in a good-sized northern, a beauty we would be proud of any other time. But not today. We wanted the big guy now.

About eight o'clock, a guy and his wife rowed over and threw in their lines. Just around the tip of the island, in sight of us.

"Heck, we don't need them around here," Marty complained. What could we do? Marty started singing. He has a lousy voice. Off key. Loud. Not getting any reaction from the intruders he sang louder. Then he stopped and asked. "Hey. Any luck?" They shook their heads and the guy's wife tried to shush us.

"No darn fish in this lake," Marty yelled. "We did better fishing the Detroit River. Any bites?" No answer. So Marty stood up and banged around and finally, considering there was a woman in the other boat, he did an inexcusable thing. He started relieving himself. "All that beer," he explained. They pulled up anchor and disappeared.

Around ten o'clock, we saw some movement in the pads. Maybe the pike. I saw him. "It's him. There!" My heart was hammering. I got the shakes. He was back.

The pike just stayed put, watching us. No matter what we cast his way, minnows, exciting artificial lures that we paid a fortune for—nothing interested him.

Marty lost his patience. "He's got to get hungry sometime.

What's he eat, anyway?" He pulled a still live minnow off his hook and tossed it toward the pike.

The minnow he threw barely touched the water when the pike lunged and gulped it down. When the water stopped boiling and rippling, we strained to see if he was still there.

"He's gone."

"No he's not," Marty pointed. The pike moved a bit farther back beneath the pads, watching us. "Here," Marty shouted, tossing another minnow in a high arc toward the pike. The water erupted as the pike flashed half out of the water, gulping the bait.

We took turns tossing minnows. What else could we do? Might as well enjoy this game.

"We gotta figure a way to outsmart him," Marty threw our last minnow in a slow arc, high above the pads. The pike lunged a good foot out of the water and sucked it in.

Marty's face showed the agony of his feelings. Awe. Bewilderment. Frustration. Then, he looked off at the sky, thinking and a happy smile slowly spread. "I know how we're going to get him."

"How?"

"You'll see. Let's go in."

Marty told me to go to our cabin and he went the other way. When he came back he was carrying something concealed in his jacket. "Tah-dah," he said. "Our newest fishing tackle."

"A gun? You crazy? Where did you get it?"

"From our trusty wood salesman."

"Rufus?"

"The same. I remember seeing it hanging over his fireplace. Kind of a beat up gun but it works. Heh-heh. Tomorrow," he winked. "We're gonna shoot ourselves a pike."

That evening, Ma Finch permitted us to build a bonfire in a pit away from the trees near the docks. We gathered around and swapped fish stories. These were experienced fishermen, including the couple we got rid of that morning. They were kind of cool towards us.

We were enjoying a crackling fire when Ma Finch came over

and sat on one of the stumps. She was good company once you got to know her.

"Hey, Ma," one of the fishermen said, "tell us again about Big Boy."

"Big Boy?" We looked at each other.

"Yeah. Haven't you heard? Ma tells a whopper of a fish story, don't you, Ma?"

"Ain't a story. It's true. Biggest fish I ever saw. Big as a sturgeon but he wasn't a sturgeon. Was a pike."

"Come on, Ma. A northern as big as a sturgeon?" one of the fishermen teased. "Biggest northern on record according to an article in a Grand Rapids newspaper, was around four feet long and weighed around fifty pounds."

"Big Boy's bigger," Ma insisted.

"You think he's still in here?"

"Nobody's seen him lately."

"Tell us about him," Marty urged. I kicked him to shut him up.

"Others have seen him from time to time and tried to hook him. One fisherman did and fought for near an hour but the line broke. Big Boy got away and was never seen since."

Rufe was listening, too. When he caught our eye he aimed, like with a rifle, and grinned. He was on to us.

We were up at dawn and rowed to our spot. Didn't even bother to bait our lines. This was going to be a toss-and-shoot game.

"Where you gonna shoot him?" I asked, shuddering at the thought of having Big Boy mangled by bullets.

"Right about here," Marty pointed for the eyes.

"You'll blow his head off. We wanna have him mounted don't we?"

"We gotta nail him first. Leave it to me," Marty growled as he loaded the rifle.

It was a long, tiring wait. We almost had company again— that couple from the other day. Marty waived at them. "Hey. Any luck?" They went the other way.

We were just about to give up for the day when the pike

appeared. Marty started being friendly. "Are you hungry, dear Big Boy? A choice morsel for your lunch?" He tossed out a large, frantically wiggling minnow toward the pike. The minnow hit the water and tried to dart for cover but the pike made quick work of him. We looked around to make sure no one was watching and tossed minnows. A little higher. A little higher. Still a little higher. The pike was in good form.

"Okay, partner. Now we get him! Just toss it high enough so I can get a good shot."

I was nervous. I was awkward. I was scared. I picked a plump minnow and looked at Marty. He winked over the rifle and aimed. "Let's go," he said. So I tossed it. High, beautifully accurate toward the pads and started to pull out of the way. But I tripped on the cooler and fell backward.

Three things happened about the same time. First, I heard the water splattering as the pike broke for the minnow. I didn't see this because I was holding on to the boat so as not to fall out. Then there was the awfullest boom of the gun echoing all over the lake. And there was the sound of splintering wood and splashing and gurgling as Marty joined me in the lake.

The boat slid under the water. Marty's hat floated by. Then he surfaced, calling me names a buddy ought not call his buddy. Far off, Ma Finche's way, came excited yelling. Boy, oh boy!

Rufe picked us up in Ma's boat. All he said was "Heh-heh-heh." A lot more gentle reaction than we got from Ma. Where in the world did that old gal pick up such colorful cuss words?

"I want you two maniacs out of here first light tomorrow. And you're going to pay for my boat," Ma screamed.

"And for my gun," Rufe added.

We packed that night also trying to use up some of our supply of booze. But after a couple of drinks, Marty took a bottle of bourbon, some glasses and told me to come along. We went to Ma's place.

"What in hell do you want here?" Ma yelled. She was madder than before.

"Want a powwow, Ma. Gotta tell you something."

She liked her bourbon neat. And we talked. Marty told her she was right about Big Boy. We saw him. Biggest pike alive. We tried every trick and it didn't work. Then Marty explained why we decided to get a gun and how I screwed up by tripping on the cooler.

"Good thing you missed. If you'd've shot him, I'd blast you myself. You dummies!"

The bourbon was going fast. Then Marty struck the deal. "One more chance to get him, Ma. Just one more." We agreed to pay her fifty for the boat we shot up and twenty-five to use her boat for just one day.

"Well," Ma said. "If you couldn't catch him already, and you couldn't even shoot him, what good is another chance? I think you goofballs just don't know how to fish."

"Look, Ma. We get enough of that crap from our wives. Just don't worry how we're gonna do it. We're gonna do it."

"All right. I'll rent you the boat on one condition."

We were all ears. "If you catch him, I don't want him hurt. You bring him in and in one piece, you hear? And then, when we see him, you let him go."

"Let him go?" Marty's voice echoed across the lake.

"Let him go!" Ma closed the book on this case.

Seemed like a no-win situation but as we thought it over, it made sense. The prize was just catching that fish. And what a business promotion it would be for her. People got a look at Big Boy, they'd be stampeding here for a crack at him. She wasn't born yesterday.

Two o'clock in the morning and we were still trying come up with a plan. I was nodding off. Then Marty was shaking me awake. "It's time, old buddy. Let's go."

We packed our stuff in Ma's boat: A gaff, a generous supply of remaining beer and booze, minnows. Then we rowed out there, not feeling enthusiastic about our chances.

We waited and drank and waited. No pike. Even if he did show up, what chance had we, anyway? We were well on our way to tying one on.

"Heck, Marty, he won't come back. After our shooting at him, he ain't stupid."

"Hic. Shuddup and pass another beer."

There were patches of fog on the water but the surface was smooth as glass reflecting the sky and trees. We rocked ever so gently. Felt like a dream!

When Big Boy showed up, we were feeling no pain. We were satisfied just looking at him. "You know," Marty said, "he likes us. Ever think about that? He likes us. So many other fishermen around and he keeps coming back to us."

"A real, true-blue friend."

Marty leaned on his elbow, holding on to his beer, and laughed. "Yeah. A real buddy." He took a sip of beer and poured some overboard an arm's length away. "A sip for me and one for my friend, Big Boy. Ha-ha."

I added my share of drink for the pike. We watched the foam spread on the water and drift toward the pike.

A fish doesn't live by drink alone, I figured. So I tossed a minnow into the foam and the pike snatched it. He didn't back away. Stayed right in that amber stream, like he was drinking it.

"Hey." Marty pointed. "He's drinking our beer." Marty took a sip and poured more into the lake. "Share and share alike," he burped.

The pike moved closer into the stream of beer. "He likes it," Marty chuckled. "Wonder if he likes booze."

"Hey, easy on my bourbon," I complained, as Marty poured a generous share into the lake. The pike got a whiff of it and, by golly, he swam into it and closer towards us. Marty poured more. He took another pull of Old Grandad Bourbon and I took a swig and we gave the pike another shot. We were all getting drunk.

Then Marty started singing. He sang and poured. Sang and drank. Sang and shared, and rippled his fingers in the stuff. The pike moved closer and closer. So close that Marty actually touched the pike's head and petted it!

After a while, it occurred to me that the fish wasn't moving. Just drifting. "Hey, Marty. Big Boy's passed out on us."

Marty pulled an oar off its lock and reached over to tap the pike. When the oar touched the pike it drifted right up to our boat. Marty yelled. "Come on, Ed. Let's haul him in."

We reached for the gaff and looked at each other. No way were we gonna stick that into him. Marty pulled out the stringer. "Here," he said. "You're closer to him."

"No way. I'm not gonna stick my hand near that mouth."

"Then I will," Marty growled. He leaned over and nudged the pike closer and reached for him. He reached too far and splashed into the lake. They both went under. When Marty surfaced he had the stringer in the pike and was handing it to me.

Big Boy came to life. Marty went under, holding on. Some times he was on the surface, gulping air, then under, blowing bubbles. I watched, fascinated, unable to react.

"What, gurgle, gurgle, are you, gurgle, watching for, dummy. Help me!" Marty shouted.

They were out of reach. I just dove in and the three of us wrestled. Half the time I was under. I wasn't a fish. I let go. When I came up, I saw Marty holding on to the stringer and the boat. The pike was jumping around like a bronco, nearly tearing Marty's arm off.

"Get in the boat and secure the stringer," Marty pleaded.

We tied the stringer to the stern ring and began rowing in. The pike pulled us one way; we rowed for dear life the other. But we were gaining. And there was a loud cheering on Ma's dock. Ma kept yelling, "Don't hurt him, dammit. Don't hurt him."

At the dock helping hands carefully hauled Big Boy out of the water, me holding his tail and Marty the front. A guy with a camera took all day setting up the picture. "Shoot, dammit," Marty yelled. That shocked Big Boy into action. He thrashed around violently. His tail slipped out of my hands. That put all the weight on Marty and he fell off the dock, letting go the stringer. Big Boy flopped around on the dock with everyone making a grab for him. Ma dove for him but all she got was the stringer which had slipped out of the pike.

Big Boy just slid into the water. He turned around, about ten feet away, and looked back at us. Marty and I were at the end of the dock getting our last look at him. Big Boy burped. Big bubbles surfaced and then he swam away.

"Damn!" Marty moaned.

"My camera! It's in the lake," the guy who was taking the picture groaned.

"You mean you didn't even get a picture?"

"It's okay, Marty," I consoled. "We caught him, anyway, didn't we? We were the only ones could do it."

"But who's gonna believe us?"

It turned awfully quiet. We just watched the wake slowly disappear.

"That was Big Boy, all right," Ma spoke up. "Beautiful, ain't he?"

"You can say that again," Marty agreed. "Hey, Ma," he put his arm around her. "Got some Old Grandad left. Interested?"

"My place," she said.

Naturally, our wives and friends didn't believe us. We tried a couple of times to find the Sunshine Cabins again but got lost in the woods. The guy who sold us the map claimed the lake we described was not the one he had in mind. He wanted to know the name of the lake. Heck, we never even got the name when we were there. Dumb!

We brooded a lot about it, Marty and me. One day my wife, of all people, saved our reputation for telling the truth about Big Boy. She handed me a copy of a Michigan sports magazine. There was a story about the largest northern pike ever caught. The fish was seventy-eight inches long and weighed one hundred and ten pounds. It was caught in Little Bass Lake in the Upper Peninsula by a Harriet Constance Finch. Bait used was Old Grandad.

IT'S NOT EASY, LOVE!

Many young married people eventually are pressured by parents and friends to have children. Not an easy decision.

He was awakened early by Carol's crying. Here was his darling wife, the beautiful, love-of-his-life, sitting on the edge of the bed, her face screwed up in torment, and tears flowing down her face.

"Sweetheart," he took her in his arms. "Why are you crying? Tell me, honey." He cuddled her as he would a helpless child, moving her blond hair away from her wet face. "What's the matter?"

He could not decipher what she mumbled through the sobs. He had never seen her like this in all eight years of their marriage. When she quieted and half-stifled the sobs, he looked into her eyes and waited for some explanation.

"Nothing," she said. "It's nothing."

"Well, if you get so upset over nothing, I hate to see the day when something really upsetting comes along. Come on, honey. What's bothering you?"

She wouldn't say. Was it pressure this time of year when all her clients wanted their tax returns done yesterday? Didn't she like the new car they had bought for her—a beautiful, white Chrysler convertible? Wasn't she feeling well? Did he say something that hurt her feelings? Had somebody else hurt her feelings?

No. Everything was fine. Great!

Twenty minutes later, after he had brewed the coffee and turned the omelet and called out to her, she appeared, dressed and carrying her suitcase. She told him she had to leave. She didn't say why, or where she was going. He watched her drive off in the morning rain, a red swirl reflecting the taillights on the glistening pavement.

When he came back inside, he smelled the burned omelet. He

dumped it, poured the coffee into the sink and decided the way his day was going he had better have breakfast at Cookie's across from his office.

What to do? He knew Carol would not run off to mother. She kept problems to herself. He decided he would, later, call her office to see if she went in. Nothing to do then but to go to work and wait this out.

The traffic was bumper-to-bumper on the freeway—a solid, three-lane line of taillights gleaming in the rain. Drivers on either side hunched over their steering wheels, tense, impatient, angry as though they had all the problems of the world on their backs. Well, *he* was the one with all the problems. His beautiful wife had left him. Not a shred of any idea why. It was so frustrating he hit his steering wheel and the horn blew. The man in the car ahead made like he was going to get out of his car and give Jim a piece of his mind. Jim held up his hands indicating it was a mistake.

He tried to reconstruct the happenings of previous days to discover what might have brought on Carol's strange mood. Nothing unusual yesterday, nor the day before. Or, going back a week, two weeks. But, a-ha! There was that slightly depressed mood he detected after they had returned from their holiday reunion at her parent's in Bethel, Vermont.

What was it she had said the day after? "What's going to become of us? Where are we going? Will we be happy when we're old and gray?" Jim was quite happy with the way their life was going already. Didn't have a care in the world. Financially sound. They were as much in love as when they married, if not more. Still made mad-passionate love several times a week, so no hang-ups there.

But she had just turned thirty-one. When he thought this bothered her, he reminded Carol that if she was old, then he was ancient being six years her senior. Yes, something was bothering her after the reunion. Carol came from a family of six children. And Jim had two brothers. With either family, a reunion made them very aware of children. Their not having any and being outspoken about not wanting any started many debates.

He and Carol had frequently talked about why not to have

children. Their careers were in high gear and getting better. They loved their freedom. There were those fantastic vacations in Hawaii. In Australia. A European tour. And there were plans for more travel. So why spoil things?

Jim's attention was yanked to the present with a jolt. The accident occurred as he tried merging off the freeway into Main Street traffic. A rusted-out, old jalopy had rammed into his door and front fender. The fender was pushed into the tire and blew it. The radiator was punctured and he could hear anti-freeze pouring out beneath.

"You asked for it," the driver of the other car shouted. He was a half-foot taller than Jim and bigger all around.

"I was merging," Jim shouted back. "You should allow merging traffic to merge, like everybody else does. What you did was stupid."

"Who you calling stupid?"

The police broke up the fight. Jim and the other driver had been rolling on the wet pavement and on the muddy shoulder, slugging it out. Jim felt his lip crack and blood trickled down his chin. His suit was soaked and caked with mud.

The police took them to the precinct.

They sat on the worn benches, waiting for the accident reports to be written up. The other driver's name was Anthony Lombardi. He sat opposite Jim, refusing to look at him. Then Lombardi walked to the pay phone and dialed. Probably was going to call his lawyer.

"No, I'm not hurt. I said I'm not hurt, all right?" Jim heard him say. "Don't worry. I'll get your brother, Harry, to give me a ride home. What? Oh, some jerk pulled right in front of me. It was his fault. What do you mean why did I get into a fight? He called me stupid so I let him have it."

Lombardi was obviously talking to his wife. "No, I don't know how much it will cost. Maybe Dad could lend us some until I get back to work. No, I didn't see Martin. How could I? I got into an accident. Don't worry. I'll see him tomorrow. I'll get the job. Don't worry." He hung up.

Jim decided to phone Carol's office. He went to the phone and searched for change. Dammit! He left it on the dresser. He put down the phone and walked back to the bench.

Lombardi had been watching. "Here," he said, flipping a quarter to Jim. "You going to get the same business from your wife?"

Jim caught the quarter. He shook his head. "No. My wife's gone. She left me this morning."

"Brother! Mine's at home. Worrying. She's the world's greatest worrier. Maybe you're lucky."

The receptionist tried Carol's line but got no answer.

"No dice?" Lombardi asked.

Jim shook his head.

"Tough." Lombardi pulled out his cigarettes and offered one to Jim.

Jim sat next to Lombardi. They were silent, brooding. Then Jim turned to Lombardi. "I couldn't help overhearing. Are you out of a job or just looking?"

"Been out of work for four months. My company laid off a bunch of us. At my age, it ain't easy getting a new job."

"You don't look too old to get started somewhere else."

"I didn't think so, but employers like younger guys. Fringe benefits cost less. I'm forty-eight. I got a problem. We still have to eat. And my wife is a worry wart."

"Got any kids?"

"Four of 'em."

"I guess it's pretty expensive, huh?"

"Nahh-h-h. You get cooked by degrees, you know? One kid, then another and another. You just keep going and never think about it. You better *not* think about it." He extinguished his cigarette. "You got any kids?"

Jim said no. He and Carol didn't realize how lucky they were. If he were in this man's situation, he'd be a basket case.

"It's too bad," Lombardi said. "It's great to have kids. It ain't easy, but I just couldn't see myself without these kids of mine. Hell! What else is there? Without kids married life could get boring as hell."

"You always wanted to have a family?" Jim asked.

"Well," Lombardi thought about it, "I guess it just happens, you know? I came from a big family. My wife's family had lots of kids. I guess it just goes on, you know?"

The sergeant approached them. "Please follow me." He had the forms to be signed. Lombardi and Jim both had said they wanted to press charges. But Lombardi looked at the papers then shook his head. "Naw, I changed my mind. I don't want to press no charges . . . if he don't."

"Neither do I," Jim said.

Lombardi shook Jim's hand. "I guess I got mad at you because I've had some problems on my mind. Any other time I wouldn't have popped you."

"Same here."

"Listen. You don't have a ride, do you? My brother-in-law's gonna pick me up. Maybe we can drop you off somewhere."

But, first, Lombardi asked his brother-in-law to stop at home to assure his wife that he was all right. Lombardi introduced Jim to his wife. She was holding a cute, dark-haired baby in her arms, and she put her free arm around Lombardi and hugged him and kissed him. "Thank God you're not hurt!" Then she turned to Jim. "Are you okay?"

Yes, Jim told her he was. He watched Lombardi sink into a worn easy chair and a little girl ran out of the bedroom and jumped onto his lap and kissed him repeatedly. "Grandpa! Grandpa!" she shouted. Lombardi looked up at Jim and smiled.

The world's going crazy, Jim thought. Kids everywhere. Everygody's having kids.

Then Lombardi said, "Mother, this poor guy's wife left him. This morning."

"Oh, that's terrible," she said. "But everything's going to work all right. Anthony and I, we've been married twenty-eight years now. We had lots of fights. But the kids made us make up."

Jim smiled. He liked this woman. She was big and certainly not the glamour type, but she wore a happy face, very warm and nice, smiling from the heart.

"He doesn't have any kids, mother."

"Well, he's young yet," she said. "Lots of time."

Jim relaxed and found himself telling them about Carol's strange behavior this morning. Carol was weepy and just packed and left him.

Mrs. Lombardi laughed. "Anthony, do you remember? I got the crying heebie-jeebies with our first child. Poor Anthony didn't know what to do. Maybe your wife is pregnant."

Jim looked at Lombardi and rolled his eyes in despair. "Well, I'd better get going," he said.

At home, Jim poured himself a drink and sat in the living room. So that was it! Carol was pregnant. And angry at him. Oh, my!

He heard the car pull into the drive. And Carol came in. "Your office told me. My God! You look terrible."

"I got into a fight. Had the stuffing knocked out of me."

"You've never done anything like this before, Jim."

"You've never left me before, either."

She put down her suitcase and approached him, shaking her head. Her warm hand felt comforting on his bruised face.

"Okay, now tell me, my runaway wife? What happened this morning?"

She sat on the edge of the easy chair and put her arm around Jim. "At first, I thought that was the only thing to do. To get away and think. But, afterwards, I realized that what I was trying to decide involved you, too."

"So you *are* pregnant?"

"Who said so?"

"Mrs. Lombardi."

"Who is Mrs. Lombardi?'

"It's a long story, I'll tell you about, later. Are you?"

"Whether I am or not is really not the issue. But, if I were, how would you feel about it?"

"Are you?"

"How would you *feel* about it? Please, Jim!"

"I'd be able to think this through better if you stopped fooling around and told me, yes or no."

"Well, imagine I *am*. And that we would have to look forward to having a child around, or two or three . . . and living on one paycheck . . . and all the risk and worry and sacrifices. How would you feel, knowing that was ahead?"

"Man! It would sure foul up the works."

"Uh-huh. That's how you feel about it!"

"Now, wait! What is, is. I may not like it, but heck, Carol, I love you and I'm sure we'd survive the ordeals somehow."

"Ordeals?"

"Dammit, Carol. You've got me confused. I don't know what to think. What in hell brought this on? You are pregnant, aren't you?"

"Every time we visit our folks, I come home feeling unsure. Scared. Wondering. All my sisters and brothers, and yours, too, have kids. You and I are the oddballs."

"So? I thought we had decided about these things already."

"I don't know about you, but every time I come back home, I have to go through the same soul searching. A lot of things come to mind. Having my brother Eddie's little Sandra in my arms. She felt so warm and soft and cuddly. Those beautiful blue eyes, so trusting and loving. I could feel her heart beat. And when she put her pudgy arms around my neck and kissed me, I didn't want to let her go."

Jim listened but said nothing. There was a faraway look in her eyes. She said, "I couldn't get that feeling out of my mind."

"Well, kids are cute at that age."

"I can still feel her in my arms. And, God! Jim, that was three weeks ago!"

"You'll get over it, honey."

"And our brother and sisters seem to be always so happy. There's all that noise and merriment around the house."

Jim held her at arms-length and asked. "Honey, are you pregnant?"

She disengaged herself from his arms and walked to the window and looked out. Long after she had let her feelings pour out, she stood there. Then she came to him. "One more time, I want to ask you."

He pulled her on his lap. Carol looked directly into his eyes. "Have you ever thought about it? *Really* thought about it? Having children?"

Sure, he had. And there were some new feelings he had while visiting with the Lombardis. There was a lot of warmth among the poverty there. But he certainly would never trade places.

"Sounds to me like you are pregnant and worried and disappointed and angry at me," he said.

"Did I say that? What I'm trying to say is that I wish there was a way that we could leave those family reunions in strength. Not with uncertainty and guilt."

"The big question, sweetheart, is 'Is she, or isn't she?' Tell me and let's get this out in the open."

"Jim, so help me! I'm going to punch you. It shouldn't make any difference either way. Don't you understand?"

"No, I don't. Help me understand."

"What I want us to feel is that we are right, whichever way. If I am pregnant then 'Great!' If I'm not, then can you look forward to life alone, just the two of us? And feel absolutely right about it? And stand there with our chins out and make clear to everyone: We have thought it over. We feel absolutely certain that this way will bring us most happiness. Most importantly, Jim, *your* happiness, too. No regrets, ever."

"I see. You aren't pregnant. You're just trying to convince yourself this is the way to go."

"I didn't say that. What I would like to know is, if I *were*, how would you react? Would you pout and worry and be angry, or would you start getting a room ready for the little one? Would you bring home books from the library about having a baby? Sign up for instructions for new parents? What if I told you, right now, start getting ready, daddy?"

"You know, this day didn't start out well. It's been lousy. And now I'm convinced. It's a terrible day."

"That's your answer?"

He paused, shook his head, slipped her off his lap and went to the bathroom. He came back with his face doctored, his hair combed and wearing fresh clothes. "Let's go," he said. "We'll use your car. Mine's wrecked."

"Go where?"

"To buy some kiddie furniture, and paint and wallpaper for the baby's room."

"Oh, Jim. I love you. You are the dearest person in the world."

"Sure, let's go."

"No. Let's stay home. I'll cook us a nice dinner, and we'll have some wine and start up the fireplace and be romantic."

"Last time around, huh? After this, romance is down and babies are up?"

"Don't spoil it."

"When is the little one joining us?"

"What little one?"

"Darn it, Carol. You are pregnant, aren't you?"

"I didn't say that."

"Then you aren't?"

"Did I say that?"

FREEDOM TREE

During a lunch break at Ross Roy a few of us went to the building's roof to enjoy a view of the Detroit River a short block away. A tiny poplar seedling grew out of a crevice in the roofing where it could not survive. An idea grew until . . .

It was eight-thirty in the morning and already a large crowd had gathered around the mammoth beech tree in front of Burning Oaks City Hall. Drivers on the Metropolitan Highway created a traffic jam as they slowed to gawk. Their attention was focused on an old man sitting on one of the large, lower branches of the tree about twenty feet off the ground. The man had hooked his cane on smaller branches to keep himself from falling. An extension ladder lay on the ground, apparently what the man had used to get up into the tree. In front of the tree was a crudely painted sign which read: "Don't Touch This Tree." Several teenagers called out to the old man. "Grandpa, please come down. You'll get hurt. Please, grandpa!"

A team of workmen wearing hard hats stood by, undecided what to do. They looked up at the man and shook their heads. Their trucks with tree-cutting equipment and hydraulic lifts were parked near the tree.

A policeman approached. "Amos, come on down," he shouted. "You're breaking the law. You'll get hurt. Let's talk this thing over. Amos? Come on down!"

"No," the old man said. "If the tree dies, I die."

The crowd separated for a city official's automobile which pulled alongside the police. It was Marvin Spitzer. "What's going on?" he asked.

"It's Amos Swift, mayor. He's up in the tree and won't come down."

"Well, you've got the equipment. Get your men up there and *bring* him down. Before he falls. We don't want to make a martyr out of him."

They started toward Amos with their hydraulic lift, but as they came near, Amos swung at them with his cane. The crowd cheered. Every swipe of his cane brought more cheers. Mayor Spitzer turned around and saw a TV news truck pull up. "Oh, for crying out loud!" he groaned. A reporter and her cameraman got out of the truck and ran to the tree.

The people now pressed around the reporter who asked questions while the cameraman shot his footage.

"What do I think?" one of the residents said. "Well, we're all for Amos Swift, but the mayor will have his way in the end, as usual. This fight over the tree has been going on for years."

They asked the mayor's opinion. "That tree is a safety hazard," he said. "Falling branches on municipal traffic could hurt somebody and get us sued. The tree's got to come down."

Amos watched the mayor being interviewed while alternately swinging his cane at the workmen who came close. "You'll never get me down," he shouted.

The battle over the beech tree had been going on long before the municipal center was built. The tree was a magnificent specimen over six-and-a-half feet in diameter, a hundred-and-fifty feet in height and its graceful gray branches spanned over one hundred feet. Although there was no exact way to determine the tree's age, arborists that Amos Swift consulted estimated it to be well over two hundred years old. Its age and size could possibly qualify it to be a National Champion American Beech, giving national recognition in the American Forester Association's National Register of Big Trees.

Amos had insisted from the beginning that the tree's beauty and importance deserved a special place in the municipal center's landscaping design. Since he had spent his entire working life as a landscaping specialist and designer, he offered his own design at no cost to the city. His plan provided ample space for the tree to stretch and grow and show off its beauty. The city planners ignored

Swift's plan and built roadways around the tree, leaving it in the center of a boulevard. Now its huge branches spread over the roads and, as Amos had expected, winter ice and snow and the high winds of spring caused branches to break and fall on the roadways. The mayor emphasized the safety problem in his campaign to have the tree cut down.

Those who knew Mayor Spitzer were convinced he was not interested in the tree one way or the other. What he wanted to make clear was who was boss in the city. It was softly spoken around town that Spitzer "owned" the city. All but one city commissioner was voted into office riding on the mayor's coattails. Appointees to the powerful planning commission and appeals board were personal friends and business associates selected by the mayor. An exception to the mayor's control was Ian MacTavish, a stubborn Scot who somehow eked out enough votes to win a seat on the city commission. And so the mayor, with his handpicked people, had his way in most city matters from their inception in the planning commission through their legislation before the city commission.

In his own right, Amos was a familiar and respected personality in the community and long before Spitzer came onto the scene. The Swifts were among the early inhabitants of Burning Oaks when it was an agricultural community forty years ago. The Swifts purchased probably the least desirable parcel of land in the northeast section of Burning Oaks. It was a ten-acre farm choked with weeds and had on it a dilapidated six-bedroom frame farmhouse that should better have been torn down to provide space for a new home than to be patched and repaired year after year. Over the years, however, the farm, affectionately known by residents as "Amos Park," was transformed. Almost every specie of tree known to the state grew on the farm as well as a variety of fragrant, blossoming shrubs and flowers. A precisely-planned and immaculately-maintained garden provided food for the Swift table with plenty to spare to be sold to passersby from the vegetable stand built in front of the home. And there were birds everywhere, nesting in the shrubbery and in the trees and feasting on rows of sunflower and berry plants.

Amos Swift's reputation grew. People pointed to him when he walked through town. "That's Amos Swift of Amos Park." College students visited Amos Park because just about every kind of tree and plant grew there which they could study. Amos had become sort of an Albert Schweitzer of living plants.

The mayor insisted that Swift was "tetched." "What is it with this guy and his damned trees? Where did he come from anyway?"

Amos was born and raised in the inner city where the homes were crammed on narrow, short lots. The homes were so close together that one could almost reach out of his window and shake hands with a neighbor. The only trees around were those planted by the city between the sidewalks and unpaved streets. Residents were poor so they used all available lot space for gardening food for their table.

When Amos was a little boy, his favorite pastime was to go to a local park to sit beneath the trees and to enjoy the space and peace. Sometimes he used money he earned from selling newspapers and running errands to pay the trolley fare to the city's metropolitan park. There he would lay on the grass beneath the trees to watch the squirrels chase each other. Occasionally, he would see a deer running free in the woods along the bridle paths and bicycle trails. He could hardly wait to get home to tell his parents about it.

"You're a dreamer," his mother had said, hugging him and looking pleased. "I wonder what you will become when you grow up."

Amos wished he had a tree of his own. He asked his father for permission to plant a tree in their yard but his father explained, "Son, there ain't room for a tree here. The shade from it would cut the sun from our garden, and we need the sun to grow our vegetables."

One day in early spring as Amos walked home from school, he saw a tiny poplar seedling growing in the crack of a sidewalk. He felt sorry for it because it could not survive without soil for nourishment. Each day when he passed this seedling he wanted to pick it up and take it with him. He decided to rescue it and replant it elsewhere. He filled a bucket with rich soil from their garden and, with a hand trowel he picked and jabbed in the sidewalk crack and extricated the tree with its roots intact. He quickly put the seedling into the soil in the bucket and brought it home, hiding it far back in their yard near the alley.

Amos feared the tree would die because most of the leaves wilted, but slowly the remaining leaves revived. The tree grew rapidly, doubling and tripling its size. His father discovered the tree one day while weeding the garden and asked Amos about it. Amos explained that he felt sorry for the tree. He planned to find space somewhere in a park for it, or even in their yard. Amos' father relented. They found space near the alley where the tree could grow and not intrude its shade into the garden.

The first thing each morning and last at night, Amos watered his tree and talked to it and admired its graceful fluttering leaves. He told his parents, "One day, when I have a home of my own, there will be lots of trees and flowers and birds."

When Amos was graduated from high school, his tree towered over the rooftops, swaying in the wind. Years after the Swifts moved away, Amos returned to admire his tree which became the largest in the neighborhood.

Because of his love for that tree and of growing things, it was natural that Amos would go into the landscaping business. At first, while a student in high school, he worked part time at a local nursery. After high school he hired on with a landscaping firm and became expert in landscape design.

The Swifts were too poor to help Amos attend college but he was able to earn enough to pay for evening classes at the junior college taking courses that helped him understand plant life. It was at school that he met and fell in love with Henrietta Brown, a music teacher. They married and lived in an apartment in the city.

Apartment life stifled Amos' spirit. He vowed to move out into the country as quickly as possible. "I want our children to have some space as they grow," he told Henrietta. On Sundays, while eating breakfast, Amos and Henrietta looked through the real estate section of the newspaper, the small farms for sale advertisements. One day Amos saw the ad: "Ten acres in Burning Oaks Village. Six-bedroom house. Needs work."

The words "Needs work" was a gross understatement. The farmhouse, built before the turn of the century, was a frame structure with a porch running three-quarters around the front. It needed paint badly. Windows were broken. The rain pipes had rusted and hung down the sides of the house. And the land was covered with a jungle of weeds and littered with junk. But Amos and Henrietta saw only the potential. Because of the poor condition, the farm's price was right.

With their savings and all the money they could borrow, Amos and Henrietta put a down payment on the farm. They moved into the old farmhouse when Henrietta was six months pregnant with their first child.

Shortly after they moved into the farmhouse, Amos discovered the huge American Beech tree. It grew on an open field several miles from the Swift farm. Amos immediately looked into the ownership of the property on which the tree stood hoping that, somehow, he could manage to buy it. He learned that the property belonged to Burning Oaks and was intended to be the future site of the municipal center.

Amos spent most of his spare time sitting beneath the sprawling branches of the tree. He brought the children to play around the tree. How fortunate that the tree was spared the woodman's ax in the rush of development in the area.

"What's the name of the tree?" Darlene, their second born, asked.

"It's an American Beech tree," Amos said.

"But has it got a name, like Jerome or George?"

The question inspired Amos to name the tree his "Freedom Tree," because it grew free and struggled for its life along with the nation, all the way back to the Revolutionary War. And so the tree came to be known as Amos Swift's Freedom Tree by family and friends.

When the Swifts moved to Burning Oaks, much of the area was zoned agricultural. There were vegetable stands along the mile roads and chickens and ducks wandered onto the roads, stopping traffic. But the rolling fields of corn and wheat and beans slowly changed to residential subdivisions and mini-malls and office buildings and factories. Then the I-75 expressway was built through the heart of Burning Oaks land.

The roar of expressway traffic replaced the sounds of birds. Fortunately, on the Swift farm, much of the traffic sounds were muted from the house by the stand of trees that surrounded it. But there no longer were chickens and ducks wandering on the roads. Three lanes of roadway ran in front of the farm with honking, impatient auto horns and the occasional whoop-whoop of police and ambulance sirens disturbing the peace.

A most shocking experience for Amos was the sudden transformation of a section of land on the Metropolitan Parkway. Amos returned from out of town one week and found most of the land north of the Parkway devoid of trees as bulldozers moved across the land knocking down beautiful oak, maple, ash, and beech trees, readying the land for the municipal center. Concrete pillars, like graveyard markers, replaced the woods.

Development encroached the very area where the beech tree stood. Plans were under discussion by the city commission for the Burning Oaks Municipal Center, including a city hall, police station, library and community center.

Amos attended every city meeting. He was shocked to see plans for a boulevard from the Metropolitan Parkway to the municipal center right through the area where the beech tree stood. Amos asked to be recognized and expressed his concern for the tree. "As you know," he said, "an important landmark stands right on the spot where you plan to pave the boulevard. You must be aware that the tree is there and should consider to plan your roads around it."

"What landmark?" one commissioner asked.

"Why the big American Beech tree. It's over two hundred years old. We're fortunate to have such a nationally-important tree on our property."

There was a flurry of discussion. The architect raised his eyebrows. Apparently he believed that the tree would just be removed for the sake of the most direct placement of roadways. They decided to study this new information.

Amos nearly suffered an emotional breakdown worrying about the tree. At every meeting where the tree might be discussed, Amos asked about the plans to protect the tree. He wrote letters to the American Forestry Association headquarters in Washington, D.C., and sent pictures of the tree and its measurements. He received appreciated responses from the Association which he read at commission meetings. The pressure from Amos at last received recognition and the architect's drawings showed the tree to be located within a boulevard. Amos shook his head in disbelief. The boulevard would accommodate the tree's huge trunk with plenty to spare, but the tree's branches would extend over and beyond the roads. He suggested that the roads by-pass the tree entirely leaving it far from the roadway.

"Look, Mr. Swift," the architect said. "You insisted that we should save the tree. So we saved the tree. That's all we're going to do."

Realizing that if he pointed out the danger from falling branches on the roads might jeopardize the tree's existence, Amos yielded. "I just want it to be on record," he suggested, however, "that I proposed isolating the tree completely from any roadway." They nodded agreement and the clerk was instructed to record Amos' opinion in the minutes.

Four years later the municipal center was completed. The tree stood in the center of the boulevard. And, as Amos had anticipated, during the winter and the high-wind season of spring, the beech tree's branches fell on the roads. It was at this point that Mayor Spitzer got involved.

Amos read about the mayor's concern in the newspaper. The city attorney indicated that the big beech tree had become a safety hazard. The mayor decreed, "That tree's got to go. It's costing too much in maintenance, and somebody could get hurt."

At this point Amos, his family, and friends circulated a petition among homeowners requesting that the city redirect its roads instead of cutting down the tree. Amos presented several thousand signatures requesting discussion of the matter at a city commission meeting. Spitzer could not ignore the number of petitioners, a substantial percentage of its total registered voters.

The commission chambers was jammed with residents when the tree discussion came up. Amos arranged for dozens of voters to rise and be recognized and state their case. Mayor Spitzer glared at them. "We're not going to take all night on this one issue. We'll allow five minutes per person for comments. Be brief and to the point."

The residents stood and made known their feelings. Finally, the mayor interrupted. "All right, we've heard enough on this matter. Since each remark is about the same, I'm closing further discussion right now." He banged his gavel.

But Amos Swift insisted on having his say. He stood in the front row, leaning on his cane. The mayor shook his head and said, "Mr. Swift, why don't you just sit down and let us get on with the city's business?"

"Mr. Mayor, I want to point out that when the roads were in the planning phase I called attention to the planning commission and architect that there was not enough room in the boulevard to accommodate the spread of the tree."

The mayor gaveled for attention. "Discussion is closed. Sit down, Mr. Swift."

Then Jerome Swift, Amos' son, stood. "Mr. Mayor, I'm an attorney representing Mr. Swift and these people. We want to place this issue before the appeals board. Furthermore, my father has the right to state his case. This is too important an issue to just shut off because it's taking too much time. The matter is on the agenda, and Mr. Swift will have his say or we may take legal action to find out why his rights to speak is restricted."

The mayor scowled and turned to the city attorney. He covered his microphone and discussed the matter then turned back to the speaker. "All right, we'll let Mr. Swift have his say but he has to keep it brief."

Amos cleared his throat several times. He had prepared notes on a ruled sheet which he held in his trembling hands. He looked at the mayor who glared at him, then the mayor scowled. "Mr. Swift, get on with it!"

"I—I don't know how to put it in words," Amos spoke hardly

above a whisper. The mayor gestured for Amos to use the microphone. Amos moved toward the microphone, leaned on his cane and cleared his throat. The mayor shook his head in disgust.

"I don't know how to put it properly in words . . . about that tree. But if you stand on Metropolitan Drive and look toward city hall and see the tree, if you have any appreciation of beauty, you have to *feel* it." His voice grew firmer now as his resolve strengthened.

"It's a rare American Beech Tree, probably the largest and oldest in our state and maybe even in the country. I talked to the American Forestry Association people in Washington and they gave me a formula that is not one hundred percent accurate but helps approximate the tree's age. Best we could figure, it's about two hundred and forty years old!" Amos looked to see what reaction this information received from the commissioners. Except for Ian MacTavish, they all looked stolidly at Amos and the mayor feigned boredom.

Amos shook his head in frustration. He was not getting through to them. "Can you imagine this? When our forefathers struggled through the Revolutionary War, this beautiful tree stood strong and free as our Constitution was created and signed. It was more than sixty years old when the British bombed Fort McHenry and Francis Scott Key wrote the words for our National Anthem. It was one hundred and fifty years old when President Lincoln signed the Emancipation Proclamation. Doesn't it pique your imagination that this tree lived through these historic times?"

The mayor checked his watch and yawned.

Amos struggled on. "I'm sure you have all read Joyce Kilmer's important poem, 'Trees'. Only God can make a tree. But it takes one mortal's mistake, a sharp saw, and down goes over two centuries of life and struggle for that tree." Amos' voice was now growing angry.

The mayor interrupted. "Would you sign a document assuming responsibility for any damage caused by falling branches from that tree? You ever lift one of those fallen branches? They weigh a ton!"

"There is no need for that to happen," Amos said.

"On, no? How would you guarantee that?"

"Change the directions of the roads. Sweep them around and away from the tree. Give it some room and peace."

"Do you have any idea how much that would cost the taxpayers? To tear up the present road, disrupt traffic while a new road is built? You may be poetic, Mr. Swift, but obviously you don't have a head for arithmetic. You're not very realistic."

"The city made a mistake. It should have a sense of responsibility and pay for that mistake," Amos said.

"*We* made a mistake? After all those hours of studying designs by the planning commission, and taking into account every problem and aspects of our designs, *we* made a mistake? Where do you come off laying the blame on us?"

"I pointed out the problem when I saw the early road designs. My statement was put into your planning commission minutes," Amos said.

"What day was that?" Spitzer asked.

Amos consulted his notes and gave the date of the planning commission meeting. The mayor spoke to the city clerk who rushed from the room. Then Spitzer said, "Our city would never get anything done if it listened to every citizen's pet peeve. Next thing you know we'll be running our roads around favorite rocks. 'Oh, please, avoid that little pond where the ducks play. Don't do this and don't do that.' We've got to do what is most efficient with the least expense to the taxpayer. Besides, I talked to the county experts on trees and they told me trees rarely lived as long as this one. It's living on borrowed time."

The mayor turned to the clerk who returned and placed papers in front of Spitzer. The mayor read the paper and looked up. "I've got the minutes for that planning commission meeting you referred to and there is nothing here showing you made any recommendations."

"But I did," Amos shouted.

The mayor handed the minutes to the clerk who ran down to Amos and showed him the copy. Amos studied it and shook his head.

"All right, we've heard Mr. Swift's and all these other comments. The discussion is over. Let's vote."

The clerk polled the commissioners. All but one voted for removal of the tree. The lone dissenter was Mr. MacTavish. The mayor glared at MacTavish and said, "Motion carried. Six to one, resolved, that we will remove the beech tree located on the boulevard for reasons of safety and costs. Next order of business is . . ."

Jerome Swift rose. "Mr. Mayor, as we stated earlier, we intend to take the issue to the city's appeals board. I trust nothing will be done until the board hears the matter."

"So be it," the mayor said. "We'll urge the board to put the issue on its agenda as soon as possible."

The appeals board heard the particulars on the tree on its next meeting, remarkable expediency. Amos and Jerome Swift presented their arguments and waited for a vote. The chairman indicated that it was the practice of the board to discuss every subject on the agenda before the people but its vote came after the chambers were emptied. This was true. The appeals board was the only body that made decisions in private.

Amos phoned the city clerk the following day to hear the decision. It was voted unanimously to let the city commission's vote stand. The tree had to go.

"When?" Amos asked.

The clerk said there was a work order for the cutting to take place within a week.

The Swift family was concerned about Amos' health. A man with a hearty appetite, Amos now hardly touched food. He slept fitfully. Henrietta had to wake him several times each night as he tossed and turned and cried out.

As the day for the cutting neared, Amos tried to organize another petition drive and take the signatures to the state capital. But everyone told Amos it was useless. Once Spitzer decided on the issue, that was the way it would go.

Now Amos put the battle for the tree squarely on his own shoulders. If ever there was a cause that he believed in, this was the one. He would save the tree or die with it. Friends sympathized with him but had no idea to what extent Amos intended to go. He asked supporters to at least be there in front of the tree on the day it was to be cut down. "Why?" they asked. "Please just be there," he pleaded. They helped carry the extension ladder for him, not sure what it would be used for, perhaps to put up the sign they helped paint for him. "Don't Touch This Tree," it said. Amos hammered the sign in front of the tree. Then he had the ladder propped against the tree and before his friends realized what he was doing, he climbed the ladder.

They watched Amos now, defying the mayor and the workmen and police. Spectators brought portable TV sets to watch local news and running accounts of the battle between Amos and the City of Burning Oaks. By mid-afternoon, reports stated that Amos Swift was weakening, and that it appeared he nearly slipped off the branch.

Jerome Swift was in court when he heard the news. He rushed to the site to see several thousand spectators milling around the tree. The harried mayor, several city commissioners, the city attorney, and police watched as another attempt to bring Amos down failed.

"Wait," Jerome shouted to the workmen. "I'm Amos' son. Let me talk to him."

A hush fell over the crowd as Jerome stepped onto the platform of a hydraulic lift and was elevated to his father's side. Jerome sat beside his father and put his arm around him. When Jerome's arm touched him, Amos wept. They heard Jerome comfort his father.

"Come on, Dad. You've done all you can. It's out of our hands now."

"Don't they understand?" Amos cried. "Why would anyone want to kill this beautiful tree? How could anyone bear seeing its arms and legs and body on a woodpile?"

Slowly they brought Amos down. He was so weak that he collapsed as they reached the ground. A hurried call for an ambulance went out. Amos lay on the ground beneath his tree, sobbing in his son's arms.

The ambulance came and they rushed Amos to the hospital. Commissioner MacTavish shook his head and gave the mayor a worried look. "You realize that the city can end up facing a hefty lawsuit if Amos dies."

"We didn't put him up in that tree. Besides, we're on record of cutting down the tree for safety reasons. Ever hear a court go against public safety?"

"But the old man warned you guys about the placement of the roadways near the tree a long time ago. He did it while you had plenty of time to do something right."

"There is nothing on record that he did."

"Well, somebody excised his statement from the planning commission minutes, but not from my log which I keep on every meeting I attend, including the planning commission and appeals board meetings that I attended," MacTavish grinned. "Lying about city records is a serious matter, Marvin."

Workmen approached the mayor. "Well, what do you want us to do now?" There was a tone of disgust in their voices.

The mayor waved an impatient arm. "Let's call it a day."

"We're not going to cut it down now?" they asked.

"You guys got a hearing problem? I said let's call it a day!"

A late afternoon sun cast a soft light on the gray bark of the beech tree. It's huge branches reached upward, like supplicating arms.

MacTavish visited Amos in the hospital. A crowd had gathered around Amos. Jerome Swift was there. Outside the room, reporters awaited word about Amos' condition.

Jerome looked at MacTavish. "Did they cut it down?"

"Not yet," MacTavish said. "You contemplating a lawsuit?"

"No chance we'd win a suit," Jerome said. "What purpose would it serve? Dad has suffered enough."

"Do it for leverage," MacTavish said.

Jerome smiled, understanding. "Have a suit pending decision on the tree?"

MacTavish nodded. "Work a trade-off. It would be a lot cheaper for the city to fix the roads than to pay, say, a couple of million dollars' judgment. Jury trial, of course."

Jerome chuckled. MacTavish stepped toward the door and asked. "Want me to plant the seed?" Jerome nodded.

MacTavish answered reporters' questions. It was too early to determine how Amos would be. Yes, MacTavish did hear some discussion of a lawsuit. How much? A couple of million dollars was mentioned.

"Two million dollars!" Spitzer groaned. "He's crazier than I thought."

"Not necessarily," MacTavish said. "I talked with our legal people and they're afraid we could be in deep trouble."

News about the battle over the tree and speculation about a lawsuit if Amos did not recover, filled the newspapers and were featured on TV newscasts.

Spitzer called an emergency session of the city commission. They discussed the possibility of a lawsuit versus the cost of rerouting the roads. He turned to MacTavish. "You're on his side on this, aren't you?"

"Mayor, my property is a couple of miles north of Amos Park where development is a bit slower. My family's been here for generations. Used to be beautiful farmland. I've seen the dozers come and lay waste to our peaceful surroundings and all those buildings go up. I can accept some of this in the name of progress. You can't halt a city's growth. But the way we've been yanking out priceless trees, well it's a damned crime. Like Amos said, that beech tree is over two hundred years old. It's the most beautiful tree I've ever seen. Why knock it down? Most cities would give a fortune to have one like it on their grounds. You guys ever poke your noses into the American Forest Magazine? Know *anything* about trees? Ever been to Amos Park?"

"Ian, get to the point. I've heard enough speeches about the darned tree," Spitzer said.

The mayor rubbed his chin, a sign that he was thinking seriously. "Anybody got ideas?" he asked. The commissioners shook their heads.

"I've got an idea or two if you care to listen," MacTavish said.

So they spared the beech tree, and rerouted the roadways using ideas Amos had submitted years ago. The tree stands free now to stretch its giant limbs, its leaves fluttering happily in the breeze.

Its huge branches spread like welcoming arms to visitors to the city. There is a strikingly-beautiful sign—gold letters on green background:

AMOS SWIFT'S FREEDOM TREE

This grand American Beech Tree (Fagos grandifolis) first saw the light of day probably in the year 1750. It was nearly 30 years old at the signing of The Declaration of Independence, and 117 years old when the Civil War ended. It is one of the oldest trees of its specie in the United States. A national treasure.

Weather permitting, the family drives Amos to the Burning Oaks City Center so he could sit beneath his tree and watch the pleased expressions on the faces of visitors.

THE PORTRAIT

What inspires an artist to paint and how could it be used in a romantic story?

He stopped often to watch Linda's house, hoping to see her but making sure she did not see him. Those who knew about Arthur's feelings about her sympathized but were frustrated and impatient with this lad who found it difficult to express himself. He was such a timid soul, and she, like him, was quiet, gentle. In this small community, everyone knew Arthur was in love with her ever since grade school. It was inconceivable that she was not aware. They passed each other with just a smile and quiet hello. If only somehow these two could be brought together.

Friends remember Arthur as a young child in school being painfully silent and when required to recite, his voice was a tremor, but what he said was quality contribution. And he had a quick pencil, racing lines upon his notebook into pleasant caricatures, images which grew in quality over the years. "He was revealing his soul," an impressed teacher once said.

Linda was also a dreamer. She took to strumming a guitar. She expressed her feelings in simple compositions and was often called upon to contribute recitals on special school occasions. Boys, even the most brazen ones who teased other girls, respected Linda's silences and walked her from school, making themselves feel special. She had plenty of suitors but took none seriously. One by one her girl friends married, among them a good number claimed they would have grabbed this Arthur because he was a nice person, serious, studious, and darn good-looking; also because Arthur was successful at the general store while continuing his education. He wanted to be an artist.

Arthur advanced his skills, taking night school classes at the community college in oil painting. A bit difficult a transition from his pencil caricatures, oils provided him more spectacular expressions. Colors excited him and what he put on canvas appeared like emotional explosions. The store owner permitted Arthur to display his paintings in a corner of the store, near the entrance, which turned out to be profitable as tourists were fascinated by Arthur's vivid landscaping colors and dreamlike scenes of people smiling happily, especially, children at play. It was a daily curiosity for townspeople to see what new paintings Arthur added to his "gallery."

Arthur's reputation as a painter grew, but it appeared any romance between him and Linda, which his many friends hoped for, was growing more unlikely. Especially after Linda served as bridesmaid for her cousin Vicky Anderson. And even more especially when Linda caught the bouquet tossed by Vicky. Not only did she catch it, she went after it like in a face-off in a basketball game. Linda was getting serious. Arthur observed and watched as a rush of available men were dating Linda.

Then a change in Arthur. Fewer paintings appeared in his gallery. Some claimed he looked ill. Linda, perhaps hearing of Arthur's condition, seemed to shop more frequently at his store. As usual, Arthur insisted on waiting on her, but his eyes now could not meet hers. Had they quarreled? How could they have since they scarcely spoke to each other.

It was commencement time at the high school again, and Linda volunteered to play an appropriate guitar rendition. It was a quaint tune, its rhythm rising and falling from near silences to bold strokes with a pleasant lilt. It was her own composition she called "Opportunity." Very well received. Some say it brought tears to Arthur's eyes.

After commencement, exciting new creations appeared in Arthur's gallery. Angels. Angels with faces resembling Linda's. Linda sitting beneath a blossoming tree in a brilliant meadow. Linda as a little child, skipping merrily along a brook. Linda floating among clouds holding a golden guitar. Was there a message here? Linda appeared embarrassed. Gossip went around. What did these angelic Linda-like paintings mean? For Arthur this was considered extremely bold.

Then the shock. The newest painting showed Linda beautiful and happy in a wedding gown alongside a groom whose face had indistinguishable features. Who was the groom? People asked Linda what she thought. She tolerated several days of gossip then marched to the store. People followed to watch. She stepped to the counter giving only a sideways glance at the painting. Arthur hesitantly walked to the counter.

Showing anger, Linda looked into Arthur's sad, pained face. A moment, then slowly a smile replaced her frown.

"I understand," she whispered. And then she said, "Yes."

Arthur removed his apron, walked around the counter to her. She smiled and he took her hand.

"Wait," she said. "I want to see it."

They paused by the painting. She nodded. "Pretty good, Arthur."

They walked from the store holding hands, whispering to each other and ignoring loud applause.

They looked good together.

ANNA

I am a senior citizen and often find myself lonely, but uncomfortable about joining a group for company. A dilemma for many seniors.

They called themselves *Senior Highs*, a club consisting of widows and widowers, divorced, and even never-marrieds, who just wanted to be with friends of their own age group. They took spirited walks in the city park, weather permitting, or in the local malls. The community recreation center provided facilities for their birthday and anniversary celebrations. Two members seemed completely out of place. There was Virgil, who the women thought was handsome but too aloof and private. And then there was Anna, sitting stiffly, so proper and shy. She appeared to be on the verge of tears with embarrassment for being there.

Once, when asked what he thought of the club, Virgil growled, "They're just a dang bunch of spouse seekers."

"Then what are you here for?"

Virgil looked away, seeming to have forgotten the question. "Too quiet at home," he said. "Too quiet."

Despite their discomfort being in the club, Virgil and Anna continued attending, neither ever sitting close to one another, and they passed by without giving the slightest hint of being aware, not even a furtive glance.

"They're made for each other," Emma Schultz insisted. She was the self-appointed club matchmaker. She contrived ways to help start them talking to each other but that only increased their embarrassment.

At the club's Valentine's dance, all eyes focused on Virgil and Anna. If ever there was an opportunity to break the ice, this was it!

But the evening wore on and Virgil and Anna just sat, detached from the merriment. Then Harley O'Connor, the most gregarious and outspoken member, decided to do something about it.

"Watch me," Harley said. "I'm gonna get Anna to dance with me and I'll take her home tonight."

"She won't dance with him," Emma Schultz laughed. "Watch her cut him down to size."

They watched Harley stride toward Anna who saw him coming and looked more frightened the closer he came to her.

Harley started off with animated conversation. No response from Anna but Virgil looked over, then quickly away. Harley asked Anna but she shook her head. He asked again and she shook her head more positively. It was no! No! Harley grabbed Anna's arm and lifted her to her feet and moved onto the dance floor.

Anna moved stiffly. Terrified. She tried holding Harley off as he danced too closely to her. Then they saw Harley whisper into Anna's ear. She jerked away and slapped him hard and rushed to the cloakroom.

Virgil watched Anna fumbling among the coats to find her wrap and then he walked to her.

"Just calm down, hear?" Virgil said. "We'll find your coat. Calm down!" His voice had risen and could be heard across the room. Anna's tear-filled eyes widened at Virgil's command. She backed away and waited.

"This it?" Virgil asked. She nodded. He held her coat and had his on the other arm.

They walked out together, not talking. Virgil took her arm to help her up and down curbs. No words appeared to be spoken.

Anna never returned to the club meetings. Virgil did, looking for Anna. At the conclusion of a meeting Virgil approached Harley.

"You proud of yourself?" he asked, moving closer to Harley with his fists clenched.

"Hey, she comes to the party, right?" Harley laughed. "What's she here for? To meet men. What else? So why play games about it."

Virgil popped Harley on the nose and marched out. Members

gathered around Harley who was bellowing and trying to stop the flow of blood from his nose.

Virgil strode to Anna's home. He knocked firmly.

Anna answered. "Yes?"

"Didn't see you at the club couple of weeks. Are you all right?"

"Yes."

"You shouldn't ought to stay away on account of Harley. Wish you would come back."

"I think not," she said.

"May I come in so we can talk about it?"

Anna hesitated but Virgil stood his ground then stepped closer to the door. She sighed and let him in.

He liked the pleasant arrangement of the living room. Colorful, comfortable-looking furniture. Flowers here and there, some real and some artificial. The room seemed to bloom with brightness.

Embarrassing silence.

It seemed obvious that Anna just did not want company so Virgil stood to go.

"No. Stay. I'm sorry. I'm just a bit . . . uncomfortable."

"It's okay," Virgil said, sitting down again in the rocker opposite the chair she sat in.

Anna made tea and put out a plate of oatmeal-raisin cookies she had baked that day. They were crisp and tasty. Virgil concentrated severely on chewing and sipping the tea, avoiding her eyes.

"You been alone long?" he asked.

"Three years. My Jim died of a heart attack."

Virgil nodded solemnly.

"But we had fifty beautiful years together." Her eyes filled.

"My Martha died six years ago," Virgil said. "I still can't handle it."

Anna looked directly at Virgil for the first time. He had light blue eyes. Bushy, very bushy eyebrows. And a mustache that was nearly snow white and scraggly. He had a full head of unruly hair that made him look cute.

"Kids?" Virgil asked.

"Two boys and a girl. They live out of state. But we are on the phone a lot. Wonderful children."

"Un-huh," Virgil acknowledged. "My Martha and I had six. The place used to jump with noise and jostling." He smiled.

"You living with the children?" she asked.

"Oh, no. Like your kids, mine are scattered to the winds. They have their own lives. We're close, though."

Virgil slowly rocked, head down, as though watching a picture screen of life playing out before him.

"Virgil?"

"Yes?" He liked the way she said his name.

"Why did you join the club?"

She ought to know, he thought. "Lonely, Anna. Got awful, depressing and lonely. Caught myself phoning the kids a lot. They were delighted to hear from me. But after a while I could tell they were busy and just being polite. And they call me. Nice to hear from them."

There seemed nothing more to say. "Well, Anna, thanks for the delicious cookies and tea." He put on his coat and moved toward the door. He paused to look at pictures on the mantle. Moved closer, nodding his head. Nice looking family. He pointed to a picture of a handsome couple.

"That him?" he asked.

"Yes. Wasn't Jim handsome?"

"Yes, he was." Virgil looked from the photo of Anna beside her husband and then back to her. "And you are still looking great, Anna."

She blushed. "Thank you."

"Look, Anna. You're all alone here. I'm gonna leave my phone number. If you need help sometimes. You never know with us old-timers. Don't hesitate to call."

Weeks passed. Virgil paced his rooms watching the phone. She would never call him. Too proud. Well, so was he.

It was mid-March. The winds howled and the rains came. Perfectly miserable outdoors. The phone rang.

"Virgil?" A quiet, frightened voice.

"Yes." His heart thumped. He adjusted the phone closer to his ear.

"This is Anna. I don't want to bother you, but all my lights and electric appliances don't work. What should I do?"

He brought along his tool kit and a pocketful of fuses and flashlight. She met him at the door, bundled in a thick, blue robe. Her face was flushed.

How helpless and vulnerable she looked, holding the light for him as he checked the fuses. She had fine hair. Very fine. And pure silver. A small, cute nose. And the cologne she wore made violin music play in his mind.

It took a while to find the trouble. When he was finished she put on a pot for tea.

He walked back home laughing, proud of himself. Lucky for him it was just a fuse. He didn't know a dang thing, otherwise.

She had smiled a lot at him. And as he was going out the front door, she squeezed his arm in thanks. He wished he could take a picture of that spot on his arm as it erupted in hundreds of thousands of goose pimples.

He felt guilty having thoughts about someone other than Martha. What would Martha think about Anna? Then he laughed. Martha would have wagged her finger at him. "Naughty, naughty, Virgil," and laugh. He wasn't being naughty. He did think very highly of Anna.

Virgil began contriving reasons to call Anna. Why not? He called to just talk. "You okay? Everything all right?"

They talked of old times. Brought lumps in his throat to reminisce.

Then came spring. The urge to see Anna overcame his shyness and he invited her to see a movie. Then they went to a play. And there were evenings when they just sat and watched TV at her place. Never at his. That would not be proper.

One evening as he was going home, Anna took his arm and looked into his eyes. She seemed to look into his very soul.

"You're a very dear friend, Virgil," she said. The smile on her face sent a pleasant ripple of feeling going through him. The room's light, from behind her, sort of crowned her hair with a halo.

He took her hands and held them and the energy flowed between them. Enough energy to light up every lamp in the house! The feeling was so powerful that he brought her toward him and planted a warm, lingering kiss on her lips.

And she thanked him!

DADDY, WAIT FOR ME

*During the Vietnam War I read accounts of Vietcong brutality
eliminating natives who were sympathetic to American soldiers.
How would sight of this affect a soldier who is a father?*

Walt lay concealed in the brush, hardly breathing, shocked by
the incredible turn of events.

Just hours ago he was thanking his lucky stars for having
survived his stay in Vietnam and awaiting the call for him to go
home at last. Then came this urgent call to action which had him
up to his neck in trouble, again.

Several yards away lay the Australian. Walt recalled their brief
conversation just before this mission started. He was a big, friendly,
cheerful man. Walt had been writing a letter to Sally and Trishia
letting them know he would soon be home. He had their picture
open before him.

"Your little girl?" the Australian had asked. He was hunched
down beside Walt, admiring Trishia's picture.

"Yes. Her name is Patricia. We call her Trishia."

"Sweet-looking little doll," the Australian said. "About three?"

"Three and a half when this picture was taken." Walt was
proud of the picture. He took it himself. He remembered the
occasion, vividly.

They were at the city park, picnicking the day before he
departed for Vietnam. He was playing "tag" with Trishia. He let
her chase him until she was about to give up. Then he stopped,
pretending to be exhausted, and she caught him, throwing her
arms around his neck and squealing with delight.

Just before he snapped the picture, Trishia was running uphill,
golden curls shining in the sun, shouting "Daddy. Daddy, wait

for me." Her arms were outstretched toward him. He took the
picture at that instant. It was a beauty.

"Lucky guy," the Australian said, breaking into Walt's reverie.
Now the Australian was dead. And Walt held little hope for
himself.

They knew this would not be an easy campaign. It was dirty
work, the worst kind, uprooting the enemy from territory the Cong
had held for years. The Cong hid in a honeycomb of tunnels so
cleverly concealed that even after an area had been apparently
cleared, the Cong would pop up and attack.

That's how it happened this time. They had advanced without
incident. Ahead, two airlifted groups snapped shut the trap. Walt
remembered that it had suddenly grown extremely quiet. Then
the air exploded with weapons firing and grenades and the Cong
all around. The trap that had been laid for the Cong was sprung,
instead, on them.

Fighting ended quickly. His company mustered a counter-
attack and broke through the ambush, but Walt, overly cautious,
held back. He lost his only chance to get out.

Now he lay concealed in a thickly-wooded area at the edge of
a small village through which they had passed. His spirits sank as
the sounds of battle grew fainter and more distant and ceased. He
was on his own.

From his position he could see the center of the village. Some
natives ventured out to see who had won then vanished into their
huts and the Cong appeared. Walt saw one then another Cong,
then more of them circling the village.

Walt shuddered knowing what would happen now. There
would be reprisals against the villagers who had aided the Americans
during their brief liberation.

The Cong leader was thin, bearded, harsh. His men scrambled
as he barked orders. Quickly they rounded up a dozen frightened
villagers. The last brought forward, Walt recognized, were the village
chief and his son.

The bearded Cong waited impassively as his men prepared for

the executions. Walt had seen evidence of atrocities before. Now he would witness them.

He heard the villagers wailing for their loved ones—the women and children huddling together, watching. Then three bursts of automatic fire ripped the air. The wailing increased as bodies fell. Walt peered through the foliage and saw the still forms lying on the ground.

Coward! He blamed himself. Do something!

The bearded one examined the bodies. Then they forced the village chief and his son to kneel. The chief looked down, awaiting the bullets. But the son looked toward the huts. In the commotion, a child came running toward him and the son warned her to go back.

The bearded one shouted an order and aimed his pistol at the child. Several villagers reached for the little girl, but she evaded their grasp.

There was something about her outstretched hands. Dark hair, not gold. "Daddy, wait for me."

Walt came to a firing position, readying his gun. Fool, an inner voice warned. Stay covered.

The little girl dodged one Cong, then another. Now she was in the clear, running toward her kneeling father. On she came with arms outstretched.

Walt fired on the run, conscious of gunfire exploding around him.

"Trishia!"

But she came on, reaching out, not aware of his pain, the searing pain Walt felt and the sudden darkness that enveloped him.

MERRY CHRISTMAS.
THIS IS A STICK-UP!

Some seniors in a nursing home I visited seemed too feisty and
mentally alert to belong there. How about a hero among them,
who could make things interesting?

The children put Mike Barnes in the nursing home because
his memory lapses resulted in several fires when food he was cooking
was left unattended. And since he had trouble getting around with
his cane, they feared he might fall and seriously hurt himself. There
was nothing wrong with his mind, however. He had a heckuva
sense of humor, a sassy disposition and belligerent pride. It was his
pride that was hurt most when the kids put him in this nuthouse.
He solemnly vowed to escape one way or another first chance.

First thing they did at the nursing home was to take away
Mike's cane because he tried to whack a couple of aides. His kids,
all six of them, now had moved out of state so he saw them
infrequently. They sold his house and put the proceeds into a bank
account drawable by any of the children for him. Sounded like a
sensible arrangement at the time.

Since Mike came to Pleasant Valley Home, the place almost
lived up to its name, thanks to Jack Smith and Frank Scannel,
Mike's two roommates. Jack liked to race through the corridors in
his wheelchair and, during visiting hours, yell with his loud,
gravelly voice, "They don't give us anything to eat here. Call the
cops!" Embarrassed aides rushed him to his room and Jack got the
attention he loved. Visitors began asking the director if what Jack
said was true. The director hated Jack, naturally.

Frank Scannel had a more devious mind. He was able to go to

the toilet by himself but he peed in his pants when Jocelyn LeBlanc was on duty and yelled for her to change him. Jocelyn was a young, shapely girl, and Frank had the hots for her.

When things got boring the boys would sneak out the front door and wander close to heavy traffic several blocks away. That drew large audiences and irate calls to the home about lax supervision.

Home director, Francine Tilley, often caught hell from Mike's children because he kept phoning them collect. The kids accepted his calls because they felt guilty about putting him in the home. Mike kept asking them to send some money. All he wanted was, say, five or six thousand dollars. With cash in his pockets he would leave this place pronto and take his buddies with him.

"What for?" the kids asked. "Why so much money?" They asked the director why Mike needed so much money? What was he up to? Francine wished she knew. She seemed on the verge of tears and dozing off losing sleep watching these three troublemakers.

One day, Mike seemed grim and silent. He stayed in his room a lot. Even the aides peeked in curious about the quiet.

"Why so quiet, Mike?" Frank Scannel asked.

"Thinking," Mike said

"About what?"

"Gettin' out of here."

Where would he go? Mike told exciting tales of Vegas, his special place. About the time he disappeared from home and his kids found him at a blackjack table with a couple of blonds on either side of him. He was smoking a cigar, a definite no-no, according to the doctor, and he was balancing a large stack of chips. "I really got that game down pat."

"The girls are beautiful there. Gorgeous." He sighed. "But my kids found me. A stupid neighbor squealed."

The Vegas tales excited Jack and Frank who volunteered to help.

It was nearing Christmas and it was cold outside. To make his break Mike would need a coat and hat. Maybe galoshes. Frank pulled off the slickest trick, copping the doctor's overcoat off the rack outside the director's office. Then Jack wheeled into their room wearing an elegant hat. Belonged to some guy who was signing up one of his family to the home and left the hat on a chair in the lobby. They hid the coat and hat among blankets in their closet.

The toy pistol came unexpectedly and put the hold-up idea in Mike's mind. They got the gun from a noisy little kid who was visiting. The kid was running around yelling "bang-bang" and Frank tripped him. The pistol flew out of the kid's hands and skidded on the floor into the wheels of Mike's chair. He dropped his blanket on it and wheeled away.

Things were falling into place. Mike had a coat, a hat, and a real-looking toy pistol. It was logical that the City Bank at the intersection a block away came to mind.

Getting out of the front door was out of the question. Everyone in the place was on alert to make sure these three troublemakers did not get out again. But there was a place in the courtyard, at the rear of the complex—that had a yard-wide hole in the cyclone fence. They had to find a way to sneak Mike into the courtyard.

Two weeks before Christmas, Mike, wearing the coat and hat and concealing the pistol, stood by the courtyard door waiting for diversions to begin. Frank and Jack got into a spirited, shouting argument with a lot of pulling and wrestling. Drew a large crowd. Mike slipped out and skippity-hopped with his walker through the hole in the fence.

At the bank a guard opened the door for Mike. Lots of people there. Mike chose a short line. He approached the teller with a note: "Merry Christmas! This is a stick-up." He showed the toy gun. The teller's eyes widened and she turned pale. She shoved the contents of her cash drawer toward Mike and fainted.

Mike struggled toward the exit past the guard who rushed to see what the fuss was about. A kindly customer held open the door for Mike and he walked out. A cab appeared and Mike hailed it.

"Where to?" the cabbie asked.

"Take me to a nice motel fast as you can."

The police captured Mike when he phoned the home trying

to make a deal—the bank's money for letting Jack and Frank out of the home. So, he was back again, in Pleasant Valley, to face a delirious Francine, who waved the local newspaper at Mike. Big headline: "Nursery Bandit Caught." A picture of Mike, smiling and giving a thumbs-up sign.

The inmates loved it. One of them escaped. And held-up a bank! Mike basked in the smiles and congratulations and swaggered as best he could swagger with his walker.

Frank and Jack scolded Mike. He should just have kept going, but a promise was a promise, Mike insisted. Next time, however, he would get farther away, fast, and work things out for his pals later. And what better time to try again than on Christmas Eve when the place was crowded and in confusion?

There was a lot of clothing laying on the couches as visitors milled around. Frank swiped a nice overcoat and Jack picked up a soft, tan shawl with matching beret. Since they took away Mike's toy gun, they had to come up with something else that appeared threatening. They stuck a roll of toilet paper in a brown paper bag with a coiled coat hanger protruding. What idiot would take that for a bomb? Well, it would have to do.

They used the same exit as the last time. At the bank, Mike went to the same teller. The note said: "Merry Christmas. This is a stick-up. There is a bomb in the bag."

The girl took the note. She looked faint and shoved the money to Mike. Before she fainted she whispered, "Good luck this time."

Outside, the same corner, Mike hailed a cab. Lots of noise was coming from the bank and Mike nervously looked down the street at the Pleasant Valley Home sign. He worked himself into the cab.

"Where to?" the cabbie asked.

This time he had to get a lot farther away. "Take me to the airport," Mike said.

In the airport souvenir shop, Mike bought a couple of cigars, for later, and a cane with a bronze eagle's head handle. He hid his walker in the corner of the store. Then he walked to the gate for his flight to Las Vegas.

The lady at the gate was a pretty thing. She smiled as she took

Mike's ticket. "Merry Christmas," she said. Seeing Mike's cane and observing his slow progress, she asked, "Need any help?"

"No, little dear," he said. "I can do very well for myself, thank you."

GOING ON

Christmas Eve for the homeless in an inner city is most demoralizing. How to make others aware?

Someone was shaking him. He opened his eyes and saw this strange face looking down at him.

"You all right, man?" the face asked.

The face had big brown eyes, several days' growth of beard and a worried expression. "You all right," the face repeated.

Ed Chalmers raised himself to his elbows and tried to clear his mind. Where was he? In an alley somewhere, he observed. Debris lay all around in the snow and he was covered with snow. And this man was trying to help him to his feet.

"Thought you were a goner," the man said. He had on a worn corduroy hat, a tattered corduroy jacket, and ancient brown pants bulky with additional trousers worn beneath. On his feet were two different kind of sneakers and a toe protruded from a hole in the right sneaker. The man leaned on a crutch made of a thick branch with a handle attached to the top with string and tape.

Chalmers struggled to his feet and staggered, trying to get the feel of things.

"Who are you?" he asked.

"Name's Duane. They call me Lame Duane," he laughed.

Ed's mind began functioning. "Well, I did it again," he said to himself. How did he get here?

"Come on," Duane said, helping Ed walk further into the alley. They struggled on the slippery snow as Duane led him to a huge cardboard structure—Sears packing cases taped together.

"Come into my palace," Duane laughed.

Inside, the floor was covered with layers of old rags. There was a musty odor from the rags and lack of ventilation, but it was considerably warmer inside.

Duane lit a candle and the place took on a homey atmosphere. On the walls were pictures of a New England autumn scene, a South Seas sunrise and at least a half-dozen pictures of clowns. Duane's face resembled the smiling clowns.

"What can I get you to drink, my man?" Duane said. "Brandy? Champagne?" He reached for a half-filled bottle labeled apple juice.

"No thanks," Ed said. "What a miserable night." He rubbed himself vigorously to get blood circulating.

"It's a beautiful night," Duane said. "You know what night this is?" There was that smile again. When Duane turned it on, an aura seemed to surround him. "Well?" Duane persisted. "Do you know what night this is?"

Ed tried to think. "What night is it?" he asked.

"Why, it's Christmas Eve. Christmas presents time, man. Time of good cheer, peace on Earth and goodwill to men. Ain't that wonderful?" A deep, prolonged laugh.

Christmas Eve, wow! How could he forget that? And here they were in some back alley sitting in a cardboard packing box. Suddenly Duane winced and rubbed his lame leg. It was thinner than the other and twisted into an odd angle. Duane saw that Ed was looking at his leg.

"Slipped off a moving freight train when I was a kid," Duane explained.

"Oh," Ed said, embarrassed.

"No problem. Got this expensive crutch my friends made for me. Get along pretty good with it."

Ed looked at the surroundings and back to Duane's leg and wondered how any human could go on like this.

Duane broke the uncomfortable silence. "You got a place to stay tonight?"

"No idea," Ed said.

"Well, then you will be my guest. And pretty soon we are going to enjoy a feast. A Christmas dinner. Delicious, hot food."

"Don't jive me, Duane. My guts are growling all over the place. Can't remember the last time I ate."

"Well, then come on. Let's go eat," Duane said. He blew out the candle and crawled out into the alley. "Come on, man."

New snow had fallen and Duane had difficulty with the slippery surfaces. Chalmers reached out to help, but Duane shrugged him off. "Don't," he said. "I can do it."

Through the snow flurries Ed could see lights of the mission kitchen ahead. People were lined up outside. Many who knew Duane called out to him.

Duane slapped hands with his friends. They made a place in the line for him and Ed. "Want you to meet my friend. He's visiting me from out of town," Duane chuckled.

Inside the mission there were Christmas decorations on the walls, small snow-sprayed trees on the tables. There was a clatter of dishes and the delicious smell of hot food.

The line moved slowly. Those waiting craned to see what food had been served to the eaters at the tables. Many of them dawdled over coffee, reluctant to go outdoors again.

Ed watched the people around him and wondered what tragic experiences dropped them into this hole of desperation. He was a long way going down. So fortunate years and years ago. Then a son lost in the war, a grieving wife who lost the will to live, and then his last child, daughter Marge, so beautiful and precious, slipped away with a whisper.

"You never know," Ed said.

"Say what?" Duane asked.

"Just talking to myself, Duane."

"Yeah, I do that a lot." There was that smile again.

A pretty girl, one of the volunteers, walked down the line saying, "It won't be long. Very soon." Must be about eighteen, Ed judged. Maybe sixteen. A lovely girl. Looked a lot like Marge when she was this age.

At last they reached the serving line. The girl stepped up to carry Duane's tray and they walked to a table. Ed paused to say silent grace then dug in. Food had never tasted this good, and he had eaten at some pretty exotic places in his time.

Ed watched the pretty girl who now moved along the tables with a steaming pitcher of coffee. She did look a lot like Marge. He tried to blot that thought out of mind.

Some of Duane's friends, now sipping their coffee, gathered around him. "Hey, Duane. What's Santa getting you this Christmas?" one asked.

"Well, let's see. I ordered a new Cadillac. Pink. With a sunroof. And a chauffeur, of course."

"Yeah, man." They were encouraging him.

"Then a nice warm home," Duane continued. "Don't have to be big. Gotta be warm, though."

"That's for sure," they agreed.

Ed watched Duane getting more and more into the spirit of it. "And I wish . . ." he paused and the smile vanished and he whispered. " . . . and I wish we be happy, all of us. If we be happy, that's all we want."

Slowly those around began to leave, patting Duane's shoulder as they passed. The volunteers were cleaning the tables for the next group. It was time to go.

Ed got to his feet. "Time to go, Duane." Duane did not move.

"Not yet," he whispered. He turned his face away from friends who might be watching. "I can't go out there."

"Sure you can," Ed said. "We can do it."

Duane looked up. There were tears in his eyes.

Ed put his arms around Duane and helped him to his feet and handed him his crutch.

Near the exit, Ed turned to look once more at the pretty young girl. She saw him and smiled. He made a peace sign and mouthed the words, "Merry Christmas." She nodded and he heard her beautiful voice above the noise.

"Merry Christmas," she said.

Then he and Duane pulled their coats around themselves and stepped out into the cold.

LAST GAME

Have no idea what inspired this story. As I awoke early in the morning in my Traverse City cabin, the words just jumped out. I went to the typewriter and in under an hour and a half it wrote itself.

An old fan claimed he saw LO way up north in Michigan's Upper Peninsula, a guy wearing a thick beard, wild look in his eyes and a familiar shrugging movement like LO was known for. How could he tell it was LO with all that beard? It was the color of it. Red. Even his top hair protruding from under an old Navy watchcap, was red. It was LO. He owned a hunk of property with hardwood trees, a hunter's log cabin and a small spring-fed pond. And there was no mistaking his dog, "Shoot," an excitable golden retriever said to have been the only thing on earth LO really loved. "Shoot" and LO. Yeah. It was LO. And when approached, LO fired angry eyes at the intruder who discovered him, and cautioned the dog. "Shoot!" he said. That's all he said, and LO and Shoot disappeared. LO is for Larry O'Reilly, a legend. And what a shame it was that he quit the game the moment of his most spectacular play. The crowd was in a frenzy as he walked off the field, out of the locker room, and simply vanished.

That was three years ago.

Some say it was a feud LO had with manager Roscoe Wilson, and maybe it was frustrated love of that beautiful blond model who dumped LO for an investment banker, just as it seemed they might get hitched. Couldn't get an answer from LO about it. He seldom talked about himself. LO put all his feelings into the game. On the field is where he talked. Quick, efficient and the only time he showed temper was as the game affected him. He had to win!

He simply refused to lose. In that sense he was not a team player. It was LO's independence that put him in Roscoe Wilson's doghouse. Even when LO won a game doing it his way, LO's way, Roscoe made it clear, "You do it my way or hit the highway." And that's what LO eventually did.

Larry, LO, was a lot of muscle gathered up in a lanky six five body. Sharp eye, and wrists that flickered the bat at the last instant to whack the cover off a ball. At bat he sat on pitches patiently and wasted no time taking cues from the third base coach as to what to do. Got reprimanded. Benched. Got a lot done his way. Three and 0 pitch. Take it? Naaah. Whack it!

Roscoe claimed LO caused him to be bald and ulcered. Just one season, Roscoe said he would tolerate this guy. But LO quit Roscoe, not the other way around, in that last game. *"The game"* they all talk about, and loved LO for.

The wonder is how LO got this high up in the game with his independent attitude. Well, wait a minute. He wasn't always that way. Not until he played for Roscoe. Most LO said about it was he hated the way the game was played now. Needed an army of different pitchers to bring in as strategy, pitch this guy different or that guy. Scout reports. Statistics. Bring in a fireballer even when the game's pitcher was doing all right. Practice films. Study batting posture. Stand this way or that way. Make a guy self-conscious instead of just whacking at a ball. "Look," LO insisted. "Give me a contract and get outta my way." LO didn't disagree with words, but when he did different than what Roscoe told him, it was like, "Oh, is that what you wanted me to do? I misunderstood." Like heck. So Roscoe benched him. The fans unbenched him. The team worshipped the guy.

Larry O'Reilly, LO, was an orphan. They say his father was a lumberman, and the woman who was his ma was just off the boat from Ireland. She died giving birth to LO. And his pa was off and away. Not an unhappy childhood for Larry, however because he was raised by a wonderful older couple named O'Reilly. That's how he got his name. They loved the kid and he them. It was the war that separated them. LO enlisted in the Navy and when the war ended, LO couldn't find the O'Reillys. He was on his own.

LO got back to playing a lot of baseball. What he was exceptional at, and gave his all to at third base. Covered a lot of ground. Smooth, effortless. A cannon of an arm. He begged for the ball to be hit his way. Looked like a little kid out there. Playing baseball was like eatin' candy. But it was at bat that endeared him. They likened him to Ted Williams. Great eye. Quick wrists that triggered his bat at the last moment when the pitch he chose to hit neared the plate.

LO spent only a little time in the minors and was called up due to a dire need for his kind of play. Near end of his last season he was batting .397 with a respectable thirty-eight homers and a hundred and twenty rbi. Considering that he was benched a lot by Roscoe, it took away possibility of LO having even more respected numbers.

Heck he knows the percentages of the game. What the odds are that LO's team could score off the pitcher. When the manager flashed a bunt sign with a man on first, nobody out and the game in a tight score, the other team never knew. Would this big guy bunt or whack the ball? Made them nervous. And with LO's long legs and his speed, they knew it didn't take much for him to beat it out.

It was a clutch game with the Yanks, that unforgettable game. The pitcher was Alex Whitcomb, a fastballer, as much as independent guy as LO was. Into the ninth inning it was a no hitter for Whitcomb, and the score tied at zero. Bottom of the ninth. No hits. No errors. Alex Brown was first up for LO's team. Alex whiffed on three pitches. Whitcomb hitched his pants and smirked as LO stepped to the plate. He had held LO to two walks and a foul out. The crowd was restless. That's when LO decided to do something about it.

The count was three balls, no strikes on LO. The guy was going to walk him! Like heck. The next pitch was a lazy curve off the plate and LO *bunted*! The ball seemed to make up its mind for Whitcomb to handle it. He couldn't. Base hit! Ruined the no hitter and Whitcomb aimed eye-daggers at LO standing comfortably on first base, looking at the pitcher seeming to say, "What're you ticked about?"

The stadium went wild. But LO was only on first base. The
way Whitcomb was pitching, LO would stay there. Not likely.
On the next pitch, which touched the dirt, LO took off for second.
The catcher, mouth open seemed to be saying, "Shit!", threw wild
to second base. The ball trickled off the second baseman's fingers,
just a little way away from the base, and LO streaked for third.
That's when Roscoe called time and made clear for LO to stay put.
Stay put! Only one out! Okay LO nodded as he hunched over
third base watching Whitcomb who was pissing-in-his-pants ticked
off.

Whitcomb threw a blazing fastball. Strike one. Randy Smith,
the batter, blinked. Where da ball go? Whitcomb grinned, spat
toward the batter. Another blazing fastball. Strike two. Whitcomb
looked at LO standing on third, and smirked. No way was he
going to let Randy Smith hit a fly ball long enough to score LO.

The catcher lazily tossed the ball back to Whitcomb who
casually stabbed at it, and it slid off his glove and fell at his feet.
LO dug his cleats into the dirt and charged for home. The noise
alerted Whitcomb, who was bending down for the ball, that
something was happening, and he heard the catcher yelling, "Throw
the ball! Throw the goddamn ball!" Which Whitcomb did. A
sizzling fastball at the catcher. The ball was coming in low to the
catcher who positioned himself about three yards in front of home
plate to block LO. The way the catcher looked at the ball coming
to him LO could see it was low. LO dove over the catcher, clear
over him. LO did a summersault and lunged for the plate. The
catcher had the ball but LO had home plate. Safe! That was the
game. Howling fans. Terrible profanity from the pitcher. Disbelief
on the catcher's face who sat on the empty base path, confused.

LO walked past all the glad hands and back patters right into
the locker room. Picked up his gear. Still in his uniform and cleats,
he walked out. Away from the stadium. Away from the game. He
disappeared. Damn him!

THANKS

For purchasing "Dying Is No Big Deal."

Also by
C. Joseph Socha
"Don't Call Me Clarence" and
"Promise"

The following are excerpts.

DON'T
Call Me
CLARENCE

A Lifelong Struggle for a
Winning Hand in Life

C. Joseph Socha

INTRODUCTION

The purpose of this book, at first, was to tell the story of my life for the family, to help them know "the old man" better. But as I moved along, it occurred to me that there are a lot of people going through the same doubts and low self-esteem that I struggled with all my life. Maybe this book could help them realize that there is a commonality to such feelings. YOU ARE NOT ALONE: Further, as I discovered the reasons I felt so "down" on myself, it helped me recover self-respect; perhaps the reader could benefit from my experience.

I believe we all have some feelings of inadequacy, a weakness that we try to hide but think that everyone is aware of. Even the most successful, outgoing people suffer some of these unproductive feelings. I remember seeing famous actors interviewed who, on stage, appeared poised and super-suave but admitted they suffered severe stage fright. Anthony Quinn, one of my favorite actors, claimed he was terrified in front of an audience. But once an actor is given a script, telling him who he was to be in a play and the words to say, he was transformed. Being somebody else hid his personal discomfort. But we are not in a play. We are always "on", at work, among friends, every moment of our daily grind.

Now, in my seventy-ninth year, I have the luxury of going back over the years, watching me perform, trying to figure me out and discovering what formed my attitude for good or not so good. I am aware of blips in my growth here and there that diminished me and some that helped me fight and change. As you read on, you may likely say, "Yea. That's what happened to me."

What a full life mine has been. I was among the fortunate who lived through the Great Depression. Fortunate to have experienced hardships that toughened my hide and made me realize that you have to tough it out on your own, not expect getting bailed out by someone else.

We are now in a new millennium. What does the future hold for me? Not much, considering life expectancy for a person my age. I'm waiting for my ticket out of here to wherever. If there is truth to this idea of reincarnation, I may turn up on Earth again. Before I go I want to thank God for giving me an opportunity to live through my country's most exciting and historic period. It's all in the history books now, but the colorful, personal experiences locked in my memory are worth revisiting.

I was a child of that Great Depression, the worst economic crisis our country faced. It was a time when, not just a person here and there was out of work, nearly the entire community was unemployed. People stayed at home, sitting on their front porches, trying desperately to control boredom and pain. They gave up electricity, relying on kerosene lanterns. They swallowed pride and applied for government food baskets when available. Then, slowly, came the WPA, FHA mortgages and Social Security. I was among the first to get a Social Security card and carry my original card in my wallet today.

We had no refrigerators. Food was preserved in an icebox with ice delivered in twenty-five-pound or fifty-pound blocks we ordered by putting a sign in the front window for the iceman to see. Melting ice dripped water to a pan beneath the icebox which we sometimes forgot to empty, and the spillover wet the kitchen floor. Meat was purchased daily from the butcher market, fresh, not frozen stiff as it is today. No doubt that's why it tasted so much better in the old days.

A peddler went through our neighborhood with his horse-drawn wagon selling fresh produce, the horse patiently waiting, swishing his tail to keep off the flies. The kids followed the peddler waiting for "it" to happen. "It" was when the horse relieved himself, embarrassing the housewives standing on the curb, waiting to make their purchases.

During tomato harvest season, farmers drove through our neighborhood with bushels and half-bushels of huge, ripe tomatoes. A bushel cost fifty cents. We ate the tomato like an apple, along with fresh-buttered bread (Oleo spread most of the time because it was cheaper). We ran through the streets eating the delicious tomato, juice squirting on our face and hands.

We bought bread, freshly-baked from the local bakery, daily after six o'clock. "Just one loaf. Pumpernickel," Mother said. I ran swift as a deer, and the nearer I approached the bakery, the stronger and more tantalizing the aroma of fresh-baked goods. The loaf, almost too hot to the touch, I cradled in my arms against my chest. The bread was unsliced. Kept fresh longer.

It seemed that summer was warmer, sunnier, longer than today's, that food tasted better and our leisure hours were more comfortable and enjoyable. There was law and order, respect for authority, more togetherness among the people because we all shared the same urgencies of existence.

Our utensils had to be scoured with abrasive powder after each meal or they rusted. Today utensils are stainless steel. No dishwashers then; we washed and wiped the dishes and put them away, taking turns as washer or wiper.

We walked to school, regardless the weather; no busses to take us as is done today. We walked to the grocery stores. There were small neighborhood stores, much like present-day party stores. Remnants of these stores are now converted to residences in the old neighborhoods. Our entertainment was provided by the local movie theatre and radio. We sat around the radio and let our minds provide the pictures imagined from the commentator's words.

There was more serious church attendance from families

who were mostly first-generation Americans, who brought their religious beliefs with them from the old country. Most interesting was the reverence shown to public libraries. We removed our hats when we went in, and our behavior was hushed inside. Respect. Much more respect.

And then came the miracles of technology. Television! Imagine, live scenes of happenings all over the world brought to us on the screen in our living room. We take it for granted today. As kids, we looked up at the moon with awe, but TV shot us right up there with our astronauts, taking man's first step on the surface of the moon.

Then the miracle of miracles ¾ the computer, with its fantastic memory, its obtrusive knowledge of our personal life. You enter your name and Social Security number and the computer lists your medical and educational history even your very personal dollars-and cents information.

There were no self-service supermarkets when I was a grocery clerk. The customer read off his list of groceries desired, I brought the merchandise from the shelves to the counter. It was talk, walk, talk walk ¾ a lot of steps and time. When the customer paid I had to calculate the correct change. Today, the check-out clerk moves the merchandise across a sensitive recorder and a computer lists the items' prices, the total cost, the cash tendered and change due. The computer also deducts from the store's inventory the merchandise sold. Not much time to visit as customers in line impatiently wait to pay and go.

Back then the typewriter was our main instrument to write copy. You made duplicate copies with carbon paper and errors had to be erased on the original and each carbon. Today, you write on a word processor and can revise copy at any time without retyping an entire document. Extra copies from the original can be made at Kinkos for mere pennies per sheet.

Progress. Lots of progress. But sometimes you yearn for the simpler old days. I have the luxury of revisiting them by just flipping the pages of this book. I can laugh about them, or cringe and kick myself. It has been a long, looooong lifetime. By and large I believe I did a pretty good job of it.

PROMISE

A Novel
By

C. JOSEPH SOCHA

CHAPTER 7

Doctor Kovacs' appointment with Professor R. Seymour at Wayne State University was for eleven o'clock in the History Department office. A secretary told him there would be a slight delay because the professor was called to an unexpected faculty meeting.

"Any idea how long the professor will be delayed?"

"I don't think more than twenty minutes. If you like we could reschedule the appointment."

"No, I'll wait," he said. "Thank you."

She handed him a cup of coffee and a publication with a marker to an article written by Professor R. Seymour, Ph.D. on *Michigan Settlements in The 1800s.*

An interesting article, he observed. Many details on the social and political developments of the City of Detroit after the War of 1812. The writing style was crisp and colorful. Credits for the professor at the end of the article were impressive.

He tried visualizing what kind of person the professor might be. Probably at least in his late forties or early fifties. Most likely he would be wearing an old, seedy suit with a vest. And he would be smoking a pipe, of course. He smiled. The old psychologist in him never quit.

"Sorry for the delay," he heard the voice that was preceded by a delicate scent of an exciting perfume. "Doctor Kovacs?"

He looked up at a strikingly attractive face. The face of a movie star he could not put a name to came to mind. Delicate features—high cheekbones, full lips, raven black hair.

"Professor Seymour?" he said. Actually, he nearly croaked the words, he was so surprised. "I was . . ."

She laughed. "You were expecting a man, weren't you? Some

crotchety old fuddy-duddy, eh?"

"Well, I er . . ."

"I suppose I should precede my name with a Ms. or Mrs. As I used to do years ago, but you would be surprised how many more calls for professional services I get since I dropped the designation."

She waited for a response, arching her eyebrows as though to say, "Well?" When he continued to stammer, she said, "My first name is Ruth. Ruth Seymour. How may I help you, doctor?"

He told her that he was working on a case involving some puzzling incidents that appeared to be about early Detroit.

She pulled a chair closer to him and looked at him intently. She certainly was an attractive woman. She wore a conservative royal blue suit, a high-neck blouse, two buttons open beneath the collar. Her skirt was a lighter shade of blue and was form-fitted and several inches above her knees.

He felt ridiculously self-conscious, and was aware, again, that the professor had repeated what he had just said, as a question.

"Early Detroit? What is so important to a psychiatrist about early Detroit history?" she said.

The perfume she wore attached its scent deep inside his nostrils. It brought feelings of *déjà vu*, soft violin music and . . .

"Doctor?" she said, bringing him back to the subject. The violins stopped playing. He looked intently into her brown eyes.

"I'm sorry," he said. "I might as well tell you that you are one beautiful woman, and I *was* expecting some seedy old fuddy-duddy, as you had guessed. You certainly aren't that. I'm as flustered as a schoolboy. How on earth did an attractive woman like you happen to get in a profession as . . ."

"As boring as history?"

"Not boring. It just doesn't fit," he said.

"What *would* fit?" she teased him.

"You could be a model, no trouble at all," he laughed. Now he was embarrassed at being too frank, at being so taken with her. "Well, I'm sure you've got more important things to do than waste it on hearing . . ."

"Flattery? No! Never too busy to hear flattery. Thank you,"

she said. "Now, you were saying . . ."

"Well, the reason I have come to you is to get some information on early Detroit history. You see, I'm a hypnotherapist, and I have a case that appears to have a problem related to an early Detroit incident. There are definite indications of there being a past-life problem of my patient."

"You think your patient has a past-life experience that is affecting his present life?" she was incredulous. "Reincarnation?"

Well, there it was! He had hoped he would not have to get into the subject. Many people had mixed feelings; some had very strong feelings, about reincarnation—about past-life experiences. It looked like she was one of them. Oh, well, he was not here to promote the idea. But he resented that amused expression on her face. He had to press on with this.

"In my initial session with my patient, while he was under hypnosis, he mentioned several puzzling incidents. He claims he saw a fort at the Detroit riverfront. He was seen by a Detroit policeman making swimming motions while lying on his stomach in his business suit along the riverfront in Hart Plaza. He told me he alternately saw the Renaissance Center buildings, then nothing but open sky in their place. In the other direction, he alternately saw the Veterans' Memorial Building, then, where the Pontchartrain Hotel is located, he saw a fort."

"He was trying to swim on the concrete?" she said.

"Yes." Kovacs almost shouted, becoming irritated with her. All he wanted was information, not ridicule. "My patient said he thought there should be water where he was trying to swim. Very confusing signals. Does any of this make sense to you?"

"Well, first of all, I find past-life experiences hard to believe. A friend of mine who went to a hypnotist, claims she was regressed to several previous lifetimes—as an Egyptian maiden in one life and as a captain of a sailing vessel in another." She shook her head. "I deal with facts. But I'll do whatever I can to help you along."

To help him along? To help him along! She would *humor* him

in his ridiculous beliefs, is what she was implying. His face flushed as he felt heat there and his nostrils quivered.

"Professor, I'm not here to convert you. The only reason I came was to get your assistance on some historical information. So let us just stick to the facts, ma'am, which you say you deal in. Just the facts."

He was embarrassed having put some temper in his remarks, but he was getting tired of all this ha-ha-ha-haing from people when past-life experiences were discussed.

"I'm sorry, doctor. I didn't mean to make light of your belief. But tell me, how *did* you, a doctor—I see you carry the M.D. designation—how did you *ever* get involved in past-life regressions?"

"Professor Seymour, don't carry on as though I'm some addle-brained, naïve person to accept reincarnation experiences. At one time, I was one of the biggest skeptics."

She directed him to a more comfortable chair and gestured to her secretary to bring more coffee.

"About ten years ago," he said, "I attended a medical convention in California and talked to several physicians who were using hypnosis for out-patient type surgery. They pointed out that some dentists were using hypnosis, too, instead of the needle."

"Oh, yes. Hypnosis is being recognized and used more and more in those ways, I realize, but . . ."

"So I attended a hypnosis training program. A few cases of past lives came up then, but I wrinkled my nose at this and said, 'Just teach me how to hypnotize.' I would use hypnosis strictly for present-life therapy."

Well, he was getting her undivided attention now. Okay, he would tell her about his most convincing past-life case. The first one. The shocker. "My first experience with a past-life situation came when I was treating a fifty-year-old woman who suffered from entomophobia—a phobic fear of insects. Nothing in her *conscious* recollection revealed causes for her condition. Then," Kovacs paused. "Look, professor, I don't think I need to justify my practice any further. Let's just get to some questions I have about my present case."

"No, no, doctor. Please! I'm very interested. Please continue about that woman who feared insects." The amused expression had left her face, replaced with a serious, pleading expression.

"Well," he continued, "the only way left for me to proceed with this woman was to ask her to go all the way back to the primary cause of her phobia."

Professor Seymour sipped her coffee and edged closer, leaning her elbows on her lovely knees.

"Suddenly, she curled up in a fetal position and her voice changed, sounding like a little girl's. Mind you this was a fifty-year-old woman. I asked her where she was. She said she was in the dark and was crying and wiping her hands, like this, over her body—like brushing things off.

"She said she was in a cellar that had a dirt floor. She had been thrown down there by her mean stepmother who was punishing her for failing to do her chores . . . and there were insects crawling all over her body. At one point she screamed and scared the daylights out of me."

"How old was she . . . in this regressed situation?"

"Nine years old. And the incident took place on a mid-western farm in the 1850s."

Professor Seymour sat back in her chair and looked off thoughtfully. "Incredible," she said. "But isn't it possible that this person was merely using her imagination and not really recalling an actual past life?"

"There are theories on both sides of this issue, professor. All I know is that I was able to bring this person to the cause of her phobia. I suggested that now that she knew what caused her fears, she should let go of the fear. Also, she must forgive that stepmother for being such a hateful person. You see, unless the patient lets go of her negative energy, her hate of the stepmother, she would not get relief. It took several sessions before she did forgive, but she did."

"She recovered?"

"Completely. And I have successfully treated many others who feared water, or heights, or had sexual problems—when we discovered that their problems had roots in some previous-life situation."

The professor was silent. Looking at him, strangely.

"So now, professor," Kovacs leaned back, "based on what I just told you about my patient's experiences at the Detroit riverfront, do you have any ideas that might help me?"

She went to a bookcase and selected a book and brought it to him. "If you are going to be dealing with early Michigan history situations, you should read this book. But this much I can tell you right away . . . from what you told me." She turned to a page of the book and pointed to an illustration of Fort Detroit. "Fort Detroit *was* located on the present site of the Pontchartrain Hotel. When your patient claimed he saw a fort in the direction of the hotel, he was at least familiar with this fact."

"What about the Renaissance Center buildings disappearing into the water?"

"Well, the original shoreline of the Detroit River during Detroit's fort days was nearer the line of the present Jefferson and Atwater Avenues. The areas that now hold the Renaissance buildings and Cobo Hall and the Veterans' Memorial Building had been filled in over the years. Much of the city's waterfront buildings are built on these filled in sites. So your patient has that about right, too."

"You say he is about right. You still believe his knowledge of Detroit's history, and not a past-life experience, is involved," Kovacs said.

"I'm sorry. You caught me pre-judging the facts," she chuckled.

Kovacs was becoming impatient with her, again. "And my patient ran into the Elmwood Cemetery where he claims he saw a terrible massacre occurring there. He said he saw a creek there running red with blood."

"Well, your patient was referring to the old Parent's Creek, a stream which exists in the cemetery today, but just a remnant of a creek. At one time, there *was* a wooden bridge over it. The creek was renamed 'Bloody Run' after a battle in 1763. There *was* an

Indian ambush there. An English force from Fort Detroit had gone on the offensive against Chief Pontiac—to raise the siege of the fort, but the Indians nearly annihilated them. The creek did run red with blood."

"Well, thank you, Professor Seymour. You have helped a great deal. May I borrow this book?"

"Certainly," she smiled. She arose and adjusted her skirt.

He was caught admiring her legs, and she did a cute hands-on-hips pose, teasing him. Embarrassed, he said, "I'll tell you one thing, professor. If the history faculty in my college days were as attractive as yours, I believe I might have majored in history."

"You make it sound like you are such an old person," she said. "You're hardly older than I," she teased.

Yes, she was certainly attractive . . . and a tease, he thought. It brought him to recall what she had said about using a Mrs. or Ms. designation before her name. Might as well find out, he decided.

"Is your husband also in education?" he asked.

"My *former* husband is in advertising."

As he was leaving, Doctor Kovacs thanked her again. She held out her hand and he took it. It was a firm handshake, but her hand was soft, and warm, and he was reluctant to let it go.

Thank you for purchasing
"Dying Is No Big Deal."
Hope you enjoyed it.

TO ORDER ADDITIONAL AUTOGRAPHED COPIES: USE
THE ORDER FORM NEXT PAGE.

TO ORDER AUTOGRAPHED COPIES:

Number of
Copies   *Price*   *Total*
_____ Don't Call Me Clarence $16.00 each $_____
_____ Promise $16.00 each $_____
_____ Dying Is No Big Deal $16.00 each $_____
           TOTAL $_____

Postage & Handling
        One book $3.50
        Two books $5.50
        ($2.00 for each additional book)

        TOTAL POSTAGE & HANDLING $_____
        TOTAL ORDER $_____

SEND CHECK OR MONEY ORDER TO:

        C. Joseph Socha
        P. O. Box 4204
        Troy, Michigan 48083

Please include your name and address, and if the autograph should
be personalized for someone special, indicate here:

_____

_____

Thank you.

BVG